Stepping Into The

FIRE

A Journal About Growing-Up
in Appalachian Ohio

STEVEN P. KELLER

Stepping Into The Fire

A Journal About Growing-Up in Appalachian Ohio

Steven P. Keller

ISBN (Print Edition): 978-1-09835-039-0

ISBN (eBook Edition): 978-1-09835-040-6

All rights reserved. No part of this book may be reproduced or transmitted in any form or by any means, electronic or mechanical, including photocopying, recording, or by any information storage and retrieval system without the written permission of the author, except where permitted by law.

© 2020 Steven P. Keller

Dedication

Every book ever written is dedicated to someone or something. This one is no different. First is my son Christopher who was intensely loved from the moment of conception whether he knew it or not. From tough and rocky times until now that love has never diminished and now as life has moved forward and as bonds have grown, I can only say I am so proud of him and his accomplishments that I could burst. I am very proud and deeply love the man he has become and cherish what he has taught me over the years.

Now comes my wife Nina who in so many ways has saved my life for more than 38 years. She is my rock and my salvation and has taught me how to receive and give love in ways I never knew possible. She has opened my eyes to endless possibilities and has led me along a path that I had never explored. It has been glorious to change in ways this old man never thought possible. She is the light at the end of my tunnel and my guide along the way.

I love you both more than you can ever know, imagine, or understand.

Many Thanks

To the individuals and groups who welcomed me to their meetings and events over the 30+ years I labored as a journalist in Southeast Ohio. Many of them I consider friends to this day. A number of them have now died, but to them and those alive I offer a debt of gratitude for allowing me to see firsthand the work they did in making our communities better places to live and work. It was their efforts that form the basis for the stories which appear in this book.

Front and back photos by Nina R. Keller

Table of Contents

A FEW INTRODUCTORY WORDS	1
STEPPING INTO THE FIRE	3
PIKE'S PEAK	6
JAKE ASBURY	13
MY AUNT MARY	16
JESSIE CALDWELL	19
SKINNY DIPPING	29
MY FAVORITE WHORE	32
THE MAN WHO SAW THINGS	53
LIFE AT THE TOP OF THE HILL	62
CHILDHOOD FRIENDS	68
SISTER MARY AGNES COOPER	72
A TIME OF BLOOD, GUTS, AND DEATH	81
KIDS I REMEMBER	86
HEAD IN A BOX	92

A FEW INTRODUCTORY WORDS

After a lot of years away from home at college and then even more time away for my first real job I came home to Ohio in 1976. I grew-up in the hills of Southeast Ohio, went to college about 40 miles away from my hometown, got one degree and began another when my dream job arose, and I and my first wife moved away from the comfortable existence of home to our new home in New York.

After more than a decade of climbing the corporate ladder and travelling the world at company expense I moved back to Ohio seeking shelter from the storm not long after the death of my mother. Most of my time in that job took me away from home which is not good for a marriage so not long after coming home a divorce took place. The most magical thing that happened in New York is that we had a son who, as the years passed, has become a most successful instructor of chemistry and is teaching future doctors what they need to know about organic chemistry. As I look back over my life, he is my crowning joy, my greatest creation. It's hard to express adequately the love that exists between a father and son because it is magical even if unseen.

I went back to college to complete my unfinished degree and taught at a small college and worked as an art therapist as my studies were taking place.

My biological father was killed at Okinawa and I never really knew him, but I know I carry some of his interests and skills. My mother eventually remarried the most wonderful man I had, and have, ever known. He had been a journalist his entire life but sold the papers he owned and retired. He was now alone which is the reason I returned to Ohio.

I grew-up in the newspaper offices he owned and learned the basics during my formative years. When I went off to college it made sense for me to study journalism, but I despised it. I have always been a blue jean and pocket T-shirt kind of guy, but the other students in the school of journalism wore suits and ties and carried briefcases. I changed majors to fine arts.

One evening while talking with my stepfather, he said the one thing he missed was writing the history of our hometown. He knew my feelings concerning journalism and some journalists, but he did not know he had thrown to me the sparks of an idea which I and others discussed. So, wearing my best pair of blue jeans and a brand-new pocket T-shirt I visited my favorite bank and bought one of the two newspapers in my hometown.

It was for him, not me, that I became a newspaper owner.

I still didn't care much for journalism, but most of the local journalists were low-key and okay. Now I had to care because I had bills and employees to pay, stories to write, and watch fondly as my father typed another of his historical pieces which he did until just five days before he died. And, in the process, I had a new wife.

I owned the paper 24 years, sold it, and continued to work for it another eleven.

In the end this is a work of fiction. Any resemblance to actual events or persons, living or dead, is entirely coincidental. And, of course, there is a great deal of elaboration.

Steven P. Keller
Ray, Ohio

STEPPING INTO THE FIRE

I grew up in a family that owned newspapers and began working in that profession, or maybe trade, when I was 11 years of age trapping rats in the large printing shop area of the business which kept the creatures from entering the office area, an event the caused most employees to have an unpleasant reaction. I was not paid for the work I did, but enjoyed the hunt, and was told my compensation was having a roof over my head and the ability to enjoy three good meals each day.

The building was one-half block in length and width with apartments on the second floor. I will never forget the smell of lead melting in the Linotype machines, oil and ink as papers were printed on a flatbed press, and now and then the smell of perfumed ink intended to give readers a pleasant surprise when they opened the pages. That special fragrance was very expensive and was kept in a safe to which I was never given the combination.

There was also the smell of sweat in the summer because at that time there was no air conditioning and in the winter the smell of gas furnaces which were worked hard to keep the old brick uninsulated structure warm.

The office area was different with a main room where typewriters were constantly click-click-clicking away and behind that front area were cubicles used by reporters as they did their journalistic chores although only one of them was in constant use – that of the sports editor. The others had become primarily used for storage or, on occasion, a space where I could go to type a story I had been assigned to do on one of several old Royal typewriters, the standard of the day.

As I grew, my job responsibilities changed to include arranging printed papers so they could be put in bound volumes, doing a variety of chores that required visiting various locations in my small hometown, and making sure all the rats were being held at bay.

In high school I began doing some writing which was strongly edited by my father to make them meet his strict standards. It was a learning process, although unpleasant at times. I was also allowed to handset some type and learn the basics of Linotype operation as well as the melting of lead for reuse in those machines. I enjoyed that work and learned more about writing in that role than I did in high school classes.

Eventually I began writing more and more stories, interviewed people, learned the operation of an old Speed Graphic camera, and decided I really did not like the newspaper business. It's not that it was boring because each day brought something new, but the routine was the same day after day, interviewing people was difficult for me because those being interviewed were often crabby and uncooperative which made the entire process unpleasant, and since the paper was a daily the schedule was hectic and when it was late being printed those who came into the office to buy a copy were more often than not simply unhappy and hard to tolerate….at least for me. I was told the customer is always right, but I didn't believe it then and still don't. BUT, you had to treat them as if they were right even if they were not.

So, as life moved forward I was graduated from high school and entered college with a major in journalism which made sense at the time. I quickly learned the world of journalism was not the world in which I wanted to live. I found the work boring, restrictive, and bothersome. I changed my major to fine arts, loved the people in that college, wore worn out pocket T-shirts and paint spattered blue jeans and for the first time in my college journey I was happy and felt at home.

I earned my BFA and began work on an MFA, but in the middle of that course of study and director of the collage called me into his office and said there was a job in New York that he considered perfect for me. If I might be interested, he would arrange an interview and in a weeks-time I was on a commercial airliner for the first time and was headed to New York. That state, I learned, was far away from the comfortable life I was enjoying in southern Ohio but I interviewed, was offered the job, accepted the offer, and began the busy chore of moving.

I spent more than ten years at that job which gave me the opportunity to see the world, to meet interesting new people, and to mature into a man. I had learned incredible lessons about life, but after more than ten years of constantly being away from home I burned out, quit that job, and moved back to Ohio where I immediately completed work on my Master's Degree and then did the unthinkable – I bought a newspaper. I didn't know it then but I was stepping into the fire.

The move was put into motion by the death of my mother. My father, actually step-father, was a journalist his entire life, had sold the newspapers he owned, and retired. As we sat together one evening and discussed death and its ramifications, he told me the one thing he missed, other than my mother, was writing the history of our hometown.

I bought a newspaper for him and joyfully watched as he did what he enjoyed most – writing the history of our town.

PIKE'S PEAK

I was saddened when learning of the passing of my old friend, Willard Pike. He was known as Willy and we had gone to school together in our small Southeast Ohio town and were graduated in the same class. After high school Willy and I took different paths. I went off to college and he became an apprentice to a locally popular and exceptionally good housepainter. Over the years, he became an accomplished painter and many homes in our hometown bear the fruits of his labor.

"Willy painted our house about 20 years ago. He scraped, and scraped, gave it a good base coat, and then two coats of the best paint he could get for us. It looks about as good today as it did the day he finished. It was an expensive job, but worth every penny," said his neighbor Jim Nickles. "I'm going to miss Willy. He was a good neighbor."

Being the same age and having many of the same interests, Willy and I went through the challenging years of growing into young men together and spent many afternoons in the treehouse, actually platform, we build in an old tree near my home. We spent some afternoons hunting chipmunks in the town cemetery, just up the street, with homemade bows and arrows. We never got one, but had a great time spent together in that pursuit and as is the case with young boys we talked about girls. We didn't know much, but knew we liked them.

His death came as a real surprise to me. He prided himself on eating right, or according to what health experts believed was right.

He exercised. Carrying long ladders and climbing up and down them can be physically challenging. He did not smoke or drink and played on a men's baseball team during the summer months. He was lean and tight, the perfect specimen of what a man headed into his senior years should be.

Then he died at the age of 57.

I lived out of town at the time of his death, but came home to attend the viewing, funeral service, and burial. Taking part in such a thing is much like attending a high school reunion. Classmates from all those years ago were there and as Willy was positioned comfortably in his coffin, we discussed the old days, things that had shaped our lives, what we were doing now, and so forth. The lies flew fast and furious. Our class had been lucky as only a handful of our classmates, four I think, had died and that included Willy. That number has now increased.

At a funeral there is sadness, of course, but some pleasure in recalling the past and things Willy and I had done, or tried to do, together. We got caught and stopped before we could pull off a panty raid in the girl's shower room during a volleyball game. Our principal gave us detention for a week but smiled as he did. He had most likely done something like that as a youth.

Or, one day we were talking philosophy in our treehouse platform when a group of four or five neighborhood thugs started to harass us. They made the mistake of gathering around the base of the tree and began throwing rocks. Willy asked, "Do you have to pee?" "Yes," I replied. "Then, let's let 'em have it" which we did and that sent them scurrying. They caught up with us later and extracted a certain price for our earlier deed. Boys, it seems, do not think of the future when acting in the present.

Or in our early days in high school when attending a local church camp we had the opportunity to see a page or two from a porn magazine. "That girl looks like Cathy Enrenrick," he said. I agreed, but the lady on those pages was much older and obviously not our classmate. Someone from the football team had brought the magazine and was happy to pass it around.

Or, during another church related excursion, one of our classmates, Jim Bethel, was known to always have gas and the power of his farts was legendary. During the prayer held at the beginning of the event, he raised himself slightly and let one go which, coupled with the fact he was sitting on an old gymnasium wooden seat, reverberated throughout the auditorium. The sound was so loud that the preacher stopped in mid-sentence, looked around, and then continued. He wanted to laugh I am sure but didn't. Willy and I couldn't contain ourselves and laughed out loud as did most of the others in the group. Except Billy Woodgear, the son of the preacher who was praying. I am sure he wanted to laugh too. If so, he did it inwardly.

Enough of the stories. The burial service was what you would expect and as those in attendance said their goodbyes to Willy and to each other many promised to keep in touch but you understood no one would. Then the cemetery where Willy and I had hunted chipmunks was empty – except for Willy, who had found his eternal home at a much too young age.

The above does not tell the rest of his story, possibly the most important part, the part that shaped his life until his final day.

* * *

When his mentor in the painting business got too old to carry ladders or paint with the precision he once did, Willy inherited the painting business. He was kept busy, made a good living, and felt this was the work he would do until the end of his career. That was until he got the job of painting Maud Campbell's old red barn which had been renovated to house several of her cattle.

As far as is known, Maude, a slim, trim 40 year old, never left town, never took a vacation, never married, and lived in the homestead in which she had been born and would likely die. Four generations of her family had lived in the home and the farm sat at the bottom of a hill along a road which ran through her property. There was a pond, two creeks which never stopped flowing, tall hills which protected her from the wind, and other than about 20 acres which served as pasture for her small cattle herd on one side of the road and another 20 acres or so on the other side of the road, the balance of her acreage was heavily forested serving as prime hunting property for her various relatives who were dedicated meat hunters and had been as long as Maude could remember.

She once told me when I returned home for a visit, "I listen to the cows making their noises and smells and I look around at all the green and am completely satisfied. Why would I ever want to leave? There is a lot of family history here. This land is in my blood, in my DNA."

Once the cost of the painting was agreed to, Willy moved his truck and equipment to a place near the barn and along with his helper, Tim McCreary, began to scrape off the lose paint in preparation for a new coat of paint. Since the barn was of fair size, 40' x 60', a week had been allotted for the scraping and other necessary preparations.

It was on one of those hot and humid days of mid-summer Willy's life changed forever.

As he was scraping paint under the roofline of the barn, he could not believe what he was seeing. "Hey Timmy, come here for a minute," he called to his helper who was working on the other side of the structure. "What's up boss," Timmy asked. "Come up this ladder and tell me what you see," Willy replied.

"Why, that's the face of Jesus. It's as plain as it can be," Tim said. "Look, there is the forehead, and there are his eyes and nose. Look there," he said pointing, "there is his mouth even a beard. It's Jesus and it's plain as day."

Willy agreed.

Many of those who live in my hometown and in the region bear the genes of the Scot-Irish tradition. One of the facets of that tradition is religion, specifically fundamentalist religion. While Willy did not practice some of the tradition such as brawling and drinking, he did attend a very fundamental church, The Church on the Hill, and had since his youth. He taught a Sunday School class, sang in the choir, and attended every church service, Sundays and Wednesdays.

My hometown sits solidly in what some call the Bible Belt, and only the very brave discredit what those church members believe. If you are not with them, you are a servant of the devil. If you had not seen the blood, you are doomed to Hell and that's forever. Even the mainstream churches are rather fundamental in their beliefs. If you live in my hometown and want to fit in you are going to attend one of the 20 or more churches, all with different names and different beliefs. There are lots of choices. Some claim if you want to go to Heaven you will attend their church and no other.

After seeing the face of Jesus and having it confirmed by Timmy, Willy came down from the ladder, sat on the tailgate of his truck, scratched his head, and knew his life was going to head in a different direction. He had received a call and he would heed it. Now, more than a painter, he was a preacher and preach he would.

Willy had only a high school education, but was bright enough to have a successful business, a very nice wife, two well behaved children, and a better than average home just a block or two from the center of the community. He had read the Bible through and through more than once and always carried one with him or in his vehicle. He knew the stories and the lessons and believed every word in the Bible was true despite science.

So, during Wednesday night services that very week he told his story and made the announcement that he was now a pastor and would like to present the sermon the following Sunday. His offer was accepted. I do not know what he said, or how he said it, but congratulations were heaped on him and after just more than a year he became the official pastor of The Church on the Hill.

This all happened when I was living out of town so I was unable to follow Willy's story day by day, but did notice publication of happenings at The Church on the Hill in the weekly newspaper I received through the mail, *The Weekly Eagle*. Willy, it seemed, was making his mark, not in the number of homes he painted, but in the number of people who changed their memberships and moved to his church, the number of people he had saved, and the number of demons he had cast out. Yes, he reportedly cast out demons.

At least once a year, sometimes twice, he held baptisms in Little Possum Creek which was one of those that ran through Maude Campbell's farm. These were major civic events with many people being dunked in the creek to rousing applause from others in the crowd including many who had brought picnic lunches and were sitting near the bank of the creek. The event was such an important community event that *The Weekly Eagle* would send a reporter and a story with photos would always follow.

I attended only one of Willy's services, a funeral for one of our mutual friends who had been killed in a car crash. I must report that Willy had the fire. During his sermon he marched, actually strutted, back and forth in front of the casket, Bible held high, and lapsed into song from time to time and the tone of his voice was loud, but controlled, as he exhorted the Devil to stay away and ordered the gates of Heaven to open for this wonderful man.

As he spoke a bass guitar began to thump out a beat, drums followed, and then dancing began with hooping and hollowing as part of it and a religious frenzy was in motion. When a familiar song I knew began I will admit I was moved to stand, sing, and dance. This was not my way, but it was that day.

Willy had changed and I cannot say it was not for the best. He was the same person with whom I had shared much of my youth, but he was more grounded, more firmly set in the person he was. My friends and classmates had a good visit after the service recalling childhood memories and embracing as I left.

I also learned The Church on the Hill had been renamed Willard's Chapel and had the largest congregation of any church in the community. Maybe it should have been renamed Pike's Peak.

I wondered as I flew back to my distant home, who had really done better in life. Me nearing the top of the corporate ladder in a distant city or Willard who stayed home and positively affected the lives of so many we both knew.

I still wonder.

JAKE ASBURY

Living in the country is a great pleasure where the daily aspects of life, devoid of the noises, smells, and requirements of a city, allow country-dwellers a kind of freedom as fresh and new as the air itself. My wife and I purchased an old farmhouse in the center of 80 acres of mostly forest and began the process of improving the house and managing the forest primarily by allowing it to do what it would do by itself. As the years passed, we met our neighbors with the nearest being about one-half mile away. In a stretch of about six miles there were only us and six other homes. There were very few people around.

If you crossed what was known as the shaky bridge there were a couple of other homes and in one of those lived the Asbury family, father Charles, mother Katherine, son Jake, and sister Abby. Jake and I had been classmates and had known each other since early childhood. They owned about 200 acres, raised a few cattle mostly as their own food source, had several garden plots one for beans, tomatoes, peppers and such, another for corn, and another for potatoes. A separate plot away from the others was an area where a variety of melons, including watermelons, were planted. Unlike me and my wife, they were true country folk. Charles inherited the land which had been in his family for more than 100 years from his father. Everything they ate came from the gardening they did, the cattle they raised, or from the animals of the forest.

They lived in the old two-story farmhouse Charles had inherited from his father and they kept it very neat and tidy inside and out. Their yard was always mowed and a small orchard they had planted near the house was always a source of good fruit and the trees were always trimmed and had been planted in neat rows. When the apples were about ready for harvest deer would come to eat those that had fallen to the ground. One or two of those orchard visitors would usually end up in one of two large freezers kept in what they called the mud room. No one in the Asbury family ever went hungry.

They didn't have much money but didn't need much. To make ends meet Charles and Jake would both work at a neighboring farm doing chores for that farmer when he needed help. On occasion both men would work for a carpenter they knew when he had a big job and needed extra manpower. They made enough to pay for insurance, fuel for farm equipment, equipment itself, some clothing and other items they could not make. When the children were small Katherine made most of the clothing they wore.

As the kids grew and achieved adulthood Abby married a young man from the area who had a similar family history as she. They bought a brand-new double wide mobile home and sat it about 50-60 yards from her family home. She and her husband had their gardens and both helped his and her families with chores when needed. The site for their new home had been made ready by Charles which was how things worked in our neck of the woods.

Early one Saturday afternoon I was returning home from a shopping trip to a nearby city when I noticed Jake was ahead of me in his old Chevy pickup he had owned since high school. You couldn't miss it with its faded paint and rust spots. He had spotted me too and stuck his arm out the window and waved. Just after we crossed the shaky bridge and made the left turn toward our road Jake suddenly stopped, got out of the truck, and ran up an embankment. I stopped too, wondering what was happening, but then Jake reappeared holding an opossum by the tail. He wacked it on the head with a hammer he got from the bed of his truck and threw the now dead animal and hammer into the truck bed.

He came to my truck and said, "There will be a possum in the pot tonight! With a few taters, an onion, and a few carrots that will be a great family feast."

And that folks is just how it is in the country.

MY AUNT MARY

I went to the funeral home today to visit my Aunt Mary who died at the age of 87. I hardly knew her because she had never been one to exhibit family values, did not connect with other family members even her two sisters, and was, in a word, toxic. There is no better way to describe her.

She also had a brother, but none of the family, blood or extended, had much to do with her. She was, however, a blood relative so I went because it seemed to be the right thing to do.

She had never been one to seek friends, not even in her younger days. After high school she attended a business college, got an associate degree, and worked at several secretarial jobs, but none of them lasted long because of her inability to work as a member of a team. There was something about her that was different, she was not happy with no apparent goals, and was described as spiteful, stand offish, and not able to work in any organized type of job so she stopped trying.

About five, maybe six, years of attempting to work she met John Witherspoon who was attracted to her pretty face and shapely body. At least she had those things going for her and after a short time the young couple married in a private ceremony.

John was a well-educated man who worked as an engineer in one of the local plants. He was not a local boy but had moved to the small city from a distant state. In their first year of marriage they had their first daughter, Emma, and then in the third year their second, Sarah. By the fifth year John left his small family saying he could no longer deal with Mary's ways, their lack of friends, and her inability to make any positive changes.

Some divorces are hard and victims of community speculation and ridicule, but not Mary and John's. People wondered how he had managed to keep the marriage together for so long. He remained in town, took care of his daughters as they grew, and ultimately took a better job out of the area. Mary was now alone as she had been most of her life, became a vicious man-hater, and taught her daughters how to be exactly like her. Emma married, but it didn't last long and Sarah didn't even try. Both girls were toxic just as their mother had taught them to be and none of them recognized family connections. I knew Emma from my work in the community, but never did have any meaningful conversations with either of the Witherspoon girls.

I had an office in the downtown center of the city and could watch as people came and went, a good pastime on a less than busy day. I would see the Witherspoon women, all three of them, walking down the street watching others who were also downtown. One would put a hand to her face to block her comments from non-family members and whispered something to the others. They were most likely criticizing the clothing worn by some or by their actions or telling a bit of gossip they had heard through the local grapevine. Sometimes you could see them laugh or make an ugly face.

They were like a cold, grey cloud even on a bright sunny day although they were always nicely and appropriately dressed which made people wonder where their money came from since Mary didn't work, and neither of the girls ever held anything other than short-term part-time jobs.

The three lived together in a small house on the west side of town, maintained their small yard, and would sit on their porch in the evening so they could watch their neighbors as they went about their chores.

There weren't many at the funeral home to honor the life of Mary Witherspoon and the girls did not stand by the casket as was the custom, but sat near the back of the parlor so they could watch, and probably criticize, those who did come. When I had viewed the corpse as long as I wanted, I started toward the back to tell the girls how sorry I was, but they had left their seats probably going to the powder room. So I left.

There are people among us who are toxic just like Mary, Emma, and Sarah Witherspoon. While they do not mix with others, they spread their toxicity among themselves, live unhappy, non-productive lives, and spread a kind of darkness which, in one way of another, affects us all.

I learned a long time ago to remain clear of such people, but to shower love upon them from afar even if that love is unwanted and rejected. It's sad really, but it takes all kinds of people to build a boat.

I did not go to the funeral service for Mary Witherspoon and from what I have been told neither did most folks, even those who shared family blood with her.

JESSIE CALDWELL

They came into the office one by one in scheduled interviews which were set thirty minutes apart. I owned a local newspaper and had advertised for a receptionist/typesetter with the position available immediately. No experience was necessary, there was no education requirement, it was a position the new person would shape according to their own desires with me saying yea or nay.

The small office was open with little or no privacy except for a bathroom located in the back. It wasn't all that private since others in the office could clearly hear what was happening in there. There were three computer stations, an area for printers, a small but adequate kitchen area with a microwave, a layout table, and a counter in the front. It was a nice building but was pretty basic although it served our needs well.

The interviews took place before mandatory drug testing and there was really no need for it. Most in our small town knew about marijuana, but nothing more powerful, so in our little town, at least back then, drugs were not the worry they are these days. If someone chose to smoke marijuana I didn't care. I was more interested in finding a person who could do the job and assist in taking the paper to a higher level.

Several interviews had been set and the applicants came on time with most being a little early which was the norm in my hometown.

The first was an attractive older lady who interviewed well but was not happy with the salary so dropped out of the competition.

The next could not speak well and did not appear to have a working knowledge of language which is important in newspaper work. The next, a young man, said he would only be there for a short time since in the next two months he would be starting a job with the state. I wished him well and said I hoped he would do well with the state and be happy.

After a couple more interviews I really did not have a clear choice of who would be hired, but there was one more to go so I kept my fingers crossed.

My town sat in the middle of the Bible Belt so churches of every description graced many streets or street corners with healthy, happy congregations which filled many of them not only on Sundays, but also on Wednesday evenings. So, when Jessie Caldwell, an attractive early thirty something with long brown hair and a long dress walked through the door I knew there was an Apostolic in the office. "I'm Jessie and I am here to interview for the position you advertised."

I went through the list of questions I had asked each candidate and she answered them well. This young woman, I thought, has a good head on her shoulders so I asked a few extra questions. She knew the language, perhaps better than me, and after looking around she said, "I think I could arrange this space a little better than it is now. I'd make it friendlier and easier to navigate through. Would that be okay?" I said it would and I could help if she was the one hired for the position. The pay was okay as were the hours and responsibilities so I explained the computer systems, the workflow, and anything else I could think of at the time. I'd let her know in the next day or so and she left.

"I don't know much about computers, but I am a fast learner and a hard worker. I can learn almost anything and I am a fast typist."

* * *

"Do you really want an Apostolic on your staff," I was asked. "That doesn't really matter to me. There is something about this lady that would fit in perfectly with the rest of us quite well. I think she is the one. She is smart, really smart."

"Well, if that is what you want. It's your business."

She was hired the following day. I gave her a key to the office, she filled out the appropriate papers, and said she would be there at 8 a.m. the next morning. After a brief explanation of how the computers and printers worked I told her where I sat, where she would sit, and where another reporter sat, and said that arrangement worked well, or at least it was what we were used to.

* * *

I usually arrived at the office earlier than the starting time so was surprised when I found her there already. Her tables, her computer and printer, had been moved to new positions and a pile of papers left in her work area had been sifted through and sorted. "Do you like it?" she asked. I said I did and was amazed she had done that work herself. "It was easy – and I have some other ideas."

I didn't know it then, but we were at the beginning of a most remarkable relationship that extended for more than the next twenty years. It was a time of learning for both of us.

"When do you get the mail? she asked.

"It's ready now."

"Want me to get it?" I gave her the box number and tossed her the keys.

When she returned with the mail it was neatly arranged in defined stacks, bills, checks, public notices, and trash. I had found the one. Or had she found me?

* * *

While Jessie did not know much about computers she was, as promised, a fast learner. The paper had several mailing lists with each having its share of problems. I left to visit advertisers one morning and returned later in the day with a notebook filled with information I needed.

"Those mailing lists…I got them fixed" she said after giving me time to settle at my desk.

"How did you do that?

"I played with them, but basically I read the directions."

"Directions?"

"Yes, there were directions. They were right on the screen."

"Well, I'll be dogged."

I will be the first to admit I have deficiencies. I am not proud of that shortcoming, but I was quickly learning Jessie could correct them, or at least correct something, when I was wrong which was more often than I would like, but that was who I was and I was at peace with that. At that early date after being hired Jessie was in the process of helping to fix me.

* * *

Every newspaper office has visitors who arrive there to pay bills, to drop off a news item, to thank us for this or that, or to complain. The complainers could, if allowed, take way too much time out of the day which did interfere with busy schedules, but was necessary even when you couldn't make them happy.

One gentleman arrived to tell me I had misspelled his name. "There are two "R's" in my last name," he said while his face was getting redder and redder.

"I'm sorry. I hate typos, but with the number of words we type every day it's amazing we don't have many more of them."

"Well, you better be careful with my name," our visitor said. "I am proud of that name."

"I will make sure that error is corrected and also watch to make sure it doesn't happen again."

"I am considering talking to a lawyer about this."

By this time my patience was being stretched so I replied, "Good. You do that but stand back because there are counter suits and I suspect one would come your way if you file. Now, I have to get to work so the door is over there and I'd like you to leave through it."

"You worthless SOB," he said as he left. I wanted to tell him the feeling was mutual but didn't.

Jessie heard the entire conversation which got loud a couple of times and said, "I sense you are a law unto yourself."

"Yes…I guess so."

That individual did not file a lawsuit and I knew he wouldn't. If I had a nickel for every time a lawsuit was threatened, I could have retired several years earlier. The worst thing that came from that conversation was that individual never spoke to me again which was more than just fine with me. I was, however, careful about the spelling of his last name when it came up in a news item which was not often. That was in accordance with good journalism and not kissing up.

"Do you get a lot of that," Jessie asked.

"I get my share, maybe more than my share, but I have yet to miss a minute of sleep. There are people who like to bitch or try to make someone else's life miserable, but that doesn't work with me."

"Can I talk to the next angry person," she asked.

"Sure. Have at it."

Others made frequent visits, some just to talk and those visits were welcomed even when we were busy.

One individual made a visit or two each week to go through our trash. He was interested in finding news releases we had trashed. He was interested in Right to Work information so once his habit was discovered Jessie would gather our two or three trash cans, put them in the bathroom, and close the door.

Or another guy would visit the day just before publication and look at every page we had laid out to get an early look at the news. When this pattern was discovered, and when she saw him coming, she would put all the pages in a box and close the lid.

All visitors were welcomed, but one became a favorite. A former high-level state employee was filled with witty and even wise statements which are remembered and quoted from time to time.

Jessie was quickly becoming the public face of the paper and what a load that lifted from me. I never did want to be a public figure, but my chosen profession had put me in that position.

* * *

When two people work back to back, no more than two feet apart, conversation between the two takes place which I suspect is normal in the workplace. Usually, it is about little things such as kids, or local events, or the latest local gossip, but sometimes it becomes more. You talk about personal things such as relationships, problems at home, dreams, challenges, etc. It is not like a husband-wife relationship, maybe more like a brother-sister thing, but it is a relationship which becomes mutually beneficial.

One day, out of the blue, Jessie said, "I have been watching how you lay out the classified page. I think I could do that."

"Have a crack at it," I said. "I'll work with you next week to see if you like it." She did that page for the next twenty or so years.

On another day, she said, "I think there is a better way to do the books. Can I look them over to see?"

"Sure. I'm not good at that sort of thing so please be my guest." That became another part of her job and she was good at it.

As an employer you like all your employees, but there are exceptions where this or that employee becomes a friend. Over the years I had two employees who fit the forever friend role and as this is being written later we, the three of us remain friends and spend time together usually over lunch at a local eatery.

Both have taught me life lessons and I hope I did the same for them. Perspectives have been changed, long held beliefs have been challenged and sometimes changed, some habits have been erased, and more than one touchy personal bias has been eradicated. It was about time, at least for me.

For many years I held a personal bias concerning education and its importance in life. I valued education almost more than anything else, but Jessie Caldwell demolished that belief, that bias. As a local girl without the financial resources within reach due to family issues she was unable to attend college, but I learned that was not due to her intelligence. She could have attended a college of her choosing because she was smart enough. Instead she chose to live life as it presented itself to her, married, had children, and when that chapter ended, she went to work.

The time she would have spent in college was short compared to the time spent raising a family and all that came with that. As time passed, she learned everything she needed to know to get along in the world which is something many college students do not learn and cannot do.

She had the uncanny ability to see a challenge before I was aware of it and when I recognized it, she would say, "I've been thinking about that. What if we do this instead?" Usually, almost always, she was right.

The list of Jessie's abilities could go on for several pages, but I've said enough. She was, in my view, the ultimate employee. The other employee, a reporter, was top notch and had been a friend long before working for me. She had marvelous word skills and over time developed her own style of writing which won many new readers and friends. Together the three of us put out a fine little newspaper and had a good time doing it. I was sitting pretty. I was blessed.

* * *

Owning a newspaper in a small town is a daunting challenge. In my town, once a thriving business center, the businesses closed one at a time often due to the retirement or death of the owner. Sometimes it was due to not enough business to keep the doors open. One particular very popular clothing business closed, and then another, and then the third, and then the final closure was announced due to the death of the owner. From my office in the center of the business district I watched as the landscape of the downtown area changed and began to deteriorate as did the buildings that once housed them.

Employee salaries are based on revenues received, so pay was never what I would have liked it to be and benefits sometimes had to be adjusted to allow for the changing times. No, or fewer, businesses amounted to less advertising, thus less operating money.

It was clear something had to change and it did.

On a grey and rainy day, I made one phone call and sold the paper. Although I would continue working for the paper the responsibilities of being the owner and paying the bills were gone. It was as if the weight of the world had been lifted from my shoulders. After twenty-four years of fighting the good fight I was tired and ready to stop throwing punches.

Since it would be several months before the changes would be fully in effect, I did not immediately tell my employees, but they noticed before too long because their pay checks came from a different source and not from me.

* * *

At about that same time Jessie was undergoing life changes on a personal level and on another grey and rainy day she said we had to talk. So, we did that day and what she had to say made me glad I had sold the paper.

"I have news," she said adding, "It's not good."

She announced she had accepted a position in another business and would be leaving in two weeks. I had hoped she would move to the new employer with me, but that would not be the case. I threw a party for her on her last day and many from the community came to wish her well and then, as I locked the door behind her, she was gone.

It was many years later I learned her real reason for leaving, but at that earlier time I was thrown into a tailspin. But important lessons had been learned and many tears, hers and mine, had been shed.

* * *

Things happen for a reason and in the end changes can be positive as they were in this case. While some changes can cause major problems, once those problems are overcome and you have recovered from the tailspin the sun shines again, but not in the same way. But the sun does shine again.

I learned to not give a single person too many responsibilities in a business because if they leave you are left hanging. My other friend, the reporter, stayed with me and together we kept the news rolling until the time we moved to a different building in a different town. Ultimately, she retired much earlier than I did to pursue other interests.

Once returning home from her more than full-time job, my wife took care of the books, collected old debts, and kept the ship afloat. She was my saving grace.

I also learned something about friendship. Even though a friend leaves you it is possible to remain friends for many years even though old hurts can take a lot of time to heal.

I learned there is a time to call some things quits. I was ready, more than ready, to call my tenure as a business owner over and it was a great feeling.

Jessie went on to move through a variety of jobs once she left the paper and then retired herself after years of hard work. She deserved her retirement and ultimate happiness.

I spent the next ten or eleven years working at the new version of the paper which I had once owned until I again felt the need to call it quits which I did. Then, I moved on to other interests which I had wanted to do for many years, but the memories of my newspaper days still linger and many of them are good, especially those of when I was the owner, publisher, and editor and the three of us worked together in a small office in my hometown.

SKINNY DIPPING

Most towns have a stream where youngsters, sometimes adults, get relief from summer heat and humidity by jumping into it. Such a place existed in a rural area outside of my hometown along a dirt road and was known as The Stones because of a massive sandstone boulder that served as a jumping off place. It had been used as a swimming hole for years and an unknown predecessor had tied a thick rope to the branch of a mighty Sycamore tree which could be used to launch swimmers well out into the middle of Possum Creek.

The water was so clear you could see the bottom of the creek and it was always fresh and clear after bypassing the old water works a mile or two away. On a hot summer day twelve or fifteen swimmers could be found at The Stones. If young ladies were swimming people wore bathing suits. If no girls were present, skinny dipping was the rule. I always wondered if girls skinny dipped if no boys were present. That's doubtful because boys were always there on a hot day. Parents did not allow their youngsters to swim there, but they did. It was a local tradition.

Most youngsters back then, in the 1950's and 1960's, had no transportation so a path had to be taken which began at the backside of the city cemetery. It was a well-known trail, wide and well worn, and care had to be taken when approaching an old sawmill which had at one time been in operation there. Legend had it that area was heavily populated by poisonous Copperheads, a much-feared snake that prospers in parts of Southeast Ohio. I never saw such a serpent there but stayed clear of the area as did most because the path was well away from it.

It was not a short walk, but on the way other items of interest could be seen such as the Devil's Tea Table, a stone pillar that rose about fifteen feet into the air. Stories of ancient people, especially witches, were told of the stone structure, but not many visited it because the path did not lead directly to it. It was just an interesting thing to see on the way to The Stones, like an automobile accident on the roadway which draws curious onlookers as they travel to a distant location.

By the time The Stones were reached those who had walked the path were more than ready to hit the cool, clear water. A survey of those present was taken and if the group was all male, the clothes came off and a plunge into the water felt wonderful and you were rapidly wiped clean of sweat and grime. You moved out of the way of others who were ready to jump into the creek and an hour or so later you were ready to sweat some more as you put on your clothes and began the trek back home.

One day my friend Willy Pike and I were swimming at The Stones, along with a small group of young men, when a car approached on the dirt road. You could hear it coming so the rule was to get down low so you could not be seen, but as luck would have it I raised up to see who was coming and discovered it was my parents who had taken the road to see if I had disregarded their message of not swimming at The Stones. My cover was blown, but they didn't stop. I could, however, see disappointment in their faces. "I guess you will get it when you get home," Willy said. "Guess so," I replied.

I did get it, but in a mild way, when I got home. I was told of the dangers of swimming in a creek because there was no life guard and you never knew what was in the water. I was reminded that one of my relatives had a swimming pool I could use. I listened, but already had plans to return there the next day with a small group of friends. We would meet in the cemetery and walk the path together. And we did.

Not long ago I returned to The Stones to see how that wonderful place was and was shocked. The water was brackish and orange as run-off from an old mine had entered it. The water was not very deep, and broken bottles and other trash littered the creek banks and the creek itself. It was no longer of any practical use at least to those who wanted to get a break from the heat of a summer day. But the rope swing was still there and helped me recall some of the most memorable, and pleasant, moments from my youth.

MY FAVORITE WHORE

Holly Nusbaugh decided by the time she was twelve years of age she wanted to become a minister. She grew up in an area of New Jersey known as The Pines on the east coast of the state. Her community was near both New York City and Philadelphia.

Her father was an ordained Presbyterian minister and served a moderately sized congregation most of whom worked in the city, New York City that is. She, her father and mother, as well as brother Nathan had a good life, were well thought of in the community, and were involved in many Christian activities which served the poor, the needy, and the castoffs of society. This is the kind of work Holly wanted to do. She felt the need to serve her fellow man.

By the time I met Holly she was in her mid to late 20's and had a most interesting story to tell. She said she often felt the need to talk and she did, actually we did. I was a good listener and, as it turned out, a good student, or at least a man willing to consider different ideas and ways of thinking.

Holly had been a bookish girl, often sitting in her room with a book in hand. She was fascinated with science and all that it was proving or disproving, with philosophy and theology, and the occasional romance novel. And then there was the Bible she had read from cover to cover more than once and the conversations she had with her father when she had a question or needed further explanation of a concept written in those biblical pages.

"I was really unsociable often sitting alone on a bench with a book in my hand," she told me. "School was boring, but I had a good collection of books on many subjects, had read them all, and was always looking for new titles. My main interest though was the Bible and its mysteries. I always found something interesting when I read it."

She breezed her way through all 12 years of public school, easily got through college with a degree in philosophy, and then it was off to seminary where at least another two years would be spent.

"I went to university and seminary in New Jersey. They were great schools and were close to home. My father had gone to that seminary, spoke highly of it, and took me on a tour of the campus. I lived on campus, but it was only an hour or so from home," she said over coffee one afternoon.

"The professors were top notch, the classes interesting and informative, and now I had a lot of new books to read. I studied hard, really hard. I learned a lot of good things, things that changed my life in one way or another, and my understanding of the world was expanded. Being away from home, not that far away but away, allowed me to feel free for the first time in my life and that felt great. It was frightening at first, but that soon passed."

After a moment she said, "There were some things I was not sure of so I asked one of my professors and he said we preach about many things that are hard to believe, but you have to believe them and always tell people to have faith they are true as laid out in the scriptures. It's faith that's important and we always have to make sure people understand that. That is what we teach."

I asked what sort of things she questioned. "You know, the virgin birth. God is powerful, but a virgin birth? The Devil and Hell. Come on. I believe in a loving God, not one who punishes and tortures people if they do what the church believes is sin. And Heaven – streets lined with gold? Really? That's not at all what Heaven is. I could go on, but are you getting my drift?" I said I was.

Holly was assigned to a small church in northern New Jersey after her graduation from seminary and began the life she had always wanted.

"The church I had was proud of its 350 members and the activities it sponsored in the community. I loved the people and I believe they loved me. I think during the two years I was there we accomplished some good things, but the questions I had while in seminary kept growing and it got to the point I had to do something different…. so I did.

* * *

In a different part of the world I was working my way up the ladder of corporate responsibility and success and, as such, had to spend a great deal of time in New York City. I had a suite of rooms near the center of Manhattan directly across from the corporate office in which I spent a lot of time. I loved New York City, especially in the evenings after work. During those times I would walk the streets, never tiring of the activity that was taking place around me.

Cops on horses chasing this or that bad guy or girl, the strange collection of people who frequented an all-night McDonald's near Time Square, people ice skating near Rockefeller Center during winter, others walking the same as me, a prostitute servicing a client in an alley, a man in a brown suit lying on the sidewalk face up clutching a briefcase, and the occasional fights seen in the side streets. It was a very different view of life for this small-town boy from Southeast Ohio.

I lived in a small community upstate near the mountains, but due to my heavy travel schedule I wasn't there much. It took a while for me to learn the downside of climbing the corporate ladder, but those lessons were being learned a little at a time.

* * *

Returning from a trip out of the country I approached my hotel and noticed a young woman standing next to the building just out of range of the streetlights. I had seen her before and figured she was one of the prostitutes who frequented hotel properties, but there was something different about her. She stood straight, not slouched like some, her clothing was not the sleazy, skimpy outfits worn by some of the girls, and from what I could see from the distance she was beautiful with raven-black shoulder length hair that was so black it looked blue when a stray ray from a street light hit it. There was a kind of class about her that I did not see in most of the other ladies of the night. I nodded to her as I entered the hotel and she nodded back.

I was only in the city a couple of days before travelling to a company office upstate and then I had the rare opportunity to be home a few days before heading out of the country again, to Mexico this time. Ten days later I returned to the city and would be there a couple of weeks before going to the airport once again to head somewhere. As I neared the door to my hotel, a female voice from behind me said, "Where have you been. I have missed you."

I turned and saw the raven-haired beauty I had noticed so many times before.

I told her I had been out of town but was in the city for a couple of weeks before heading out again.

"My name is Ruby. What's yours?" she asked. I told her my name and said I wasn't looking for whatever it was she might be offering. "I'm not offering anything," she replied. "I've watched you walking at night for a long time and thought it might be time we got better acquainted as friends."

"That's a good idea," I said. "I'm away from home and other than my peers at the company I don't have any friends here. I could use a good conversation from time to time."

"Let's do that then," she said after looking at her watch. "I have to go now, but I'll catch up with you later."

I nodded in agreement and entered the hotel for a night of rest. But I had a warm feeling, the kind that comes when you make a new friend. I didn't know it then, but that evening began several years of discussion which changed my life and perceptions in many ways and I hope I helped change hers as well.

* * *

We talked once or twice a week when I was in the city. Spring was coming and one warm evening Ruby asked if I wanted to walk to the square - Time Square. I said sure. "I'm not working tonight," she said, "so we can have a good talk. I have a story I'd like to tell you."

As we walked she took my hand. I looked at her surprised. "When friends walk and talk there is nothing as important or as meaningful as direct human touch. Does this bother you?" I replied it didn't so we kept walking, hand-in-hand, toward the square. We could see Radio City Music Hall and then Rockefeller Center, St. Patrick's Cathedral and then turned toward the bustling square.

As we approached the square, a police officer walked toward us on his evening beat. He was twirling a night stick in cadence with his every step, almost like a drum major leading a band.

"Good evening, Ruby," he said. "It's a good night for a walk."

"Yes it is," Ruby replied. "Joe, I'd like you to meet my friend Steve. He's from Ohio."

"Ohio huh? I've never been there. Should I make a trip someday?"

"I live in the southeastern part which is heavily forested with steep hills. It really is beautiful there with streams, wildlife, and a quiet, peaceful lifestyle. You should visit someday."

"Thanks for the invite. Got to keep moving," Joe said and walked on. He looked back. "You be safe Ruby."

"You too Joe," Ruby said and we kept walking the last block or so.

"You and Joe seemed very friendly," I said. "Yes, we are old friends. Sometimes I help the police. I'll tell you about that later."

* * *

You can always find a place to sit in Times Square. We chose two benches which faced each other and watched the crowd as it moved around going nowhere in particular. "I've got a story to tell you," Ruby said.

As she looked at me I noticed her eyes were so black the reflections from them were clear and sharp. They were incredibly black and when she looked at me it was as if she were looking into my soul. She wore little or no makeup except for a hint of a pale lipstick. She didn't need eye makeup since her eyes were so strong. There was something special about this young woman. I just didn't know what it was yet, but I would soon find out.

I value my education and those who made my educational journey a pleasure and a time of discovery. I value my days as a professional in New York and all that came from that time and after. But what Ruby was to tell me would challenge much of what I had been taught, would make me a better, more tolerant man, and would open doors that otherwise would never be opened. I sat quietly and listened.

* * *

"I am a prostitute. You know that or at least suspect it. But what you don't know is that I am also an ordained minister," she said while looking at me straight in my eyes.

"A minister…but…."

"Yes, I know what you are thinking. Yes, I am a minister, ordained and licensed."

"And, by the way," she added, "my real name is Holly, Holly Nusbaugh."

She told me of her time in college and in seminary and the time she had a church in New Jersey. She also explained that her father, a minister, and mother had raised her according to their Christian values and were strict, not only in their beliefs, but in the upbringing of their children.

"I still believe in the strength of my religion, but I have many questions," she said. "Sin…is there really such a thing? The virgin birth… really? Hell, I do not believe there is such a place and there is no Devil or Satan, only deeply rooted human temptations. I believe in a loving God, not one who would send people to a place like Hell. I do not believe we were born in sin, only with lessons to learn. I think being born again is a silly idea. Why return to childhood just so you can enjoy the benefits of a religion? Most of that is about control…. the control of the church over the people it serves. It's about building congregations and making money. The church says it deals with spirituality, but it doesn't. It deals with religion and those two concepts are not the same."

I nodded but sat silent and continued to listen.

She said as a girl and as a young woman she had felt the desires of human sexuality but did not explore or experiment. "A preacher's daughter getting pregnant or being considered promiscuous would have been a sticky place to be. I know it happens, but not in my family. When I went off to seminary I was a virgin, but not when I left."

She said there were study groups in seminary and her study partner was a young man named Ryan. "We were both virgins and we discussed that now and then so after a time we decided to do some experimentation and we did, time and time again. I realized how much I liked the process, the act, and Ryan did too. We both felt so much better after being together, so much closer, almost as if we were one. I had never felt that way before and I began to realize the power of sex, but that was not something I felt comfortable doing when I had my church so here I am. I am happy. I do not feel humiliated or used. I do not feel like a slave. I do not feel as if I am in danger or that I am dirty or a slut. I have learned sex and love are two very different things."

After a few moments she said, "What I am doing actually makes some people feel better after being with me and that's what the words of the Bible are supposed to do, but don't."

"So explain to me about your friends in the police department," I said. "Prostitution is illegal isn't it?"

"Yes it is," she replied. "The police in the area know about my double life. When they have a need for a minister or counselor, they pretend to arrest me, take me to the station, and then I work with the officer or the victim as a counselor and then they let me go. In both cases, doing the work of a prostitute and/or as a counselor, I am helping to satisfy basic human needs in a way I never felt before. I feel as if I am doing the work I was intended to do."

* * *

Holly and I had conversations for several years and many of them changed my views about life, religion, and the future. The changes I felt were greater than hers because she was strongly grounded, had solid beliefs, but was always willing to listen to a different point of view. I do not know if anything I offered changed her, but our conversations certainly changed me.

"What do you think of the church in general," she asked one evening. I said I had been raised a Methodist in a small church and felt weekly services were important for some people for social interaction, if no other reason. "Where I come from our heritage is mostly Scots-Irish and we still hold on to that heritage," I told her.

"I grew up a Presbyterian and still am," Holly said. "Methodists and Presbyterians are very similar with only small differences, so small that they really are insignificant. I think as long as you believe in a supreme being and honor that presence you are on solid ground. I often wonder why we have so many churches when there is only one supreme God-energy. People leave a church to create a new one because of petty arguments or disagreements about this or that theological idea. It is really silly and unnecessary, but people will do what they will do, right or wrong. We do have free will."

She continued. "In seminary we had several classes dealing with church finances which were considered mandatory and important. I agree finances are important, but not to the detriment of the spiritual realm. Churches in every community have financial needs. A church has to maintain its creature comforts, has bills to pay, sometimes has a house where the minister and his family live, the minister's salary, and so forth. Religion is high maintenance which is why we stress the importance of financial support."

"You mentioned the spiritual realm. Isn't that the same as religion," I asked.

"No. the two are very different. Religion is going to church, listening to a few Bible verses and a sermon, putting in a donation when the offering plate is passed aisle to aisle, and then going home after the service is done. You will do the same thing every week."

She thought for a moment and said, "Spiritually is truly the heart of every life, but people confuse the two and feel if they go to church they are getting a dose of spirituality. They are not."

"Explain," I commented.

"There is a supreme being, but it is not a person with flowing white hair sitting on a throne somewhere. I see it as an energy which controls everything and you can tap into it through prayer or meditation. Within that energy is everything you ever need to know. You just have to ask. You pay for religion through your tithes and offerings. Spirituality is free to every living being, but you don't hear that in seminary or in the vast majority of legitimate organized religions. Churches want and need your money to keep operating. It's almost as if they are less concerned with your soul."

From time to time she would be silent and a look would come over her face which made me feel she was getting information from a source I could not see.

"Let me go deeper," she said after a moment. "We call that energy God for lack of a better term. We are taught there is God, then comes Jesus whose death released our sins, and for many people Jesus is God. Excuse the language, but that is a load of crap. People need something to believe in so they believe in the teachings they hear in church. That's the easiest thing to do and their minister would not steer them wrong. Right?"

I agreed.

"This has been the Christian teaching for hundreds of years and during that time the church has dumbed us down all for the sake of larger congregations and more money. Religion is all about money. Most ministers who have been trained, educated, and ordained through a seminary are good people, but they are operating in an atmosphere of mainly myth, even if they have silent, personal, and unstated or unspoken beliefs. They bow to the power of the big church organization which is not about saving souls, but about making money."

After another moment of silence, she said, "I was not born with a load of sin that needed to be forgiven and neither were you or anyone. I had lessons to learn and some of them came from church, but certainly not all."

With the changing of the seasons and a cold wind and grey skies, she said, "I'd like to continue this further, but not tonight," she said. "I'll talk to you later," and she was gone.

* * *

Fall turned to winter in New York with frigid temperatures, more snow than anyone wanted or needed, and limited highway travel. For me that meant trips to distant lands, many of them warmer, and less time in New York City. For Holly that meant business as usual and we did not have another conversation for nearly a month, maybe two, but on one cold winter night she invited me to her apartment, near where I stayed, and we had more conversation along with a cup or two of tea and some homemade chocolate chip cookies.

Her apartment was not like ones portrayed in movies where prostitutes live in humble, if not deplorable, conditions. It was beautiful with nice furnishings and lots of light and bookshelves on almost every wall filled with books of every description including various reprints of the Bible as well as art, history, poetry – well, about everything.

"I don't invite many people to my home," she said. "I really don't have many friends and of the ones I have I don't want them to know too much about me. I am a very private person. By the way, that photo over there, they are my parents, and the one hanging on the wall is my brother. He is just about out of my life. He moved to the west coast to work for a law firm there. I hardly ever hear from him or him from me. That's about all the family I have. My father died not long ago after a life spent in the ministry and mom, well she is in a nursing home due to dementia. That's tough, but I see her every week and she just keeps failing. Sometimes she doesn't know who I am. That's really hard, but I belief that is the path that has been predestined so I accept it, usually with a smile on my face. She offered wise advice my entire life, but now I can't offer her that same consideration."

"I'm sorry," I said, "about your parents, but your home is beautiful."

"I've done well and I am proud of that. I wanted to invite you here because we are friends and I have more to say to you. You have told me about issues with your family due to your absence and all I can say about that is for you to know that your future will be what it will be, but I think you have learned that climbing the corporate ladder is not all it is cracked up to be."

I agreed.

"You may have wondered if I am safe in doing what I do. Yes, I am. I am very selective in who I spend time with and am good at judging personalities when I see a person I find attractive. Some people might call me a high-class whore, but I think of myself as a high class person."

"I am glad you feel you are safe and you have obviously done well. That makes me happy. By the way, I agree you are a high-class person – and a good friend. You have made my times alone here in the city enjoyable."

"When we last talked I spoke about myth, and Jesus, and religion in general. I sense you will be leaving before too long and wanted to fill you in what I was talking about. I believe you will return to greener pastures, to Ohio, and that many changes in your life lie ahead. Embrace them, learn from them, and go forward. Whatever those changes are, they have been laid out for you. Believe in them and trust."

"Yes, I am considering going back to Ohio to see where life leads me. It seems as if I need a change. My schedule is hectic and takes me away from family and friends way too much. I want a quieter life, one I direct not what I am directed to do by others. I value your words of wisdom."

"Okay, here we go. First, religion and its teachings are based on myth, not necessarily historical fact. Jesus may be the son of God, but so are you and so am I. Jesus may have been a great teacher and he might have been inspired because he found the secret of how to tap into the God-energy I told you about. We don't need saved, we just need to remember."

"So, if I learn to get to that spiritual energy everything I need to know will be given to me if I just ask?"

"Right. Prayer and meditation are the keys to the kingdom, so to speak."

"Okay. Tell me more."

"Sincere prayer can be meditation. Sit alone, close your eyes, and let the answers come as they will. Listen closely and do this every day. You may be surprised how your life will change. You spend a lot of your time on airplanes. That's a good place to do this."

In a moment she said, "Go to church if you wish because it won't hurt and don't toss your Bible away because there are some good lessons in it, but remember it has been rewritten and rewritten and edited and edited to increase the belief in the teachings of the church. It's not worthless but put up your filters of reason to sift through the stories. It can be a good read."

"What else do you want me to know?"

"I believe there is a very strong and vital unseen world and there is much to be learned by exploring it. That will come with time, but when it does believe it is there and it can help you."

"I can believe that, but I wonder what about you? What is your future?"

Gazing at the pictures on the wall she said, "I miss my family, but I know they are no longer available to me. I am getting older and in a few years I will have to quit this work because my looks will fade and I will no longer be attractive to potential customers. I believe in cutting losses before they become fact. In a way, I am a scholar and have much to teach, perhaps at the university level. I don't know for sure only that my time doing this work will come to an end sooner rather than later and I am okay with that."

I asked if she would ever consider marriage and having a family.

"Are you proposing?" she asked

"No. I was just curious."

"I don't think I would consider that. I am far too independent, far too self-centered, and far too interested in walking my own path in life. I find warmth in my recollections of family life during my upbringing, but that is not for me. I want to grow old with more good memories than bad."

I looked at my watch. "I have to go since I have an early flight in the morning, but this has been beyond wonderful. Thank you and you will always be in my memory."

"Good night my friend," she said as I got my coat and walked toward the door. We hugged, she kissed me on the forehead, and I walked away and down the hall to the stairs which led to the ground floor and to the door. With hesitation I walked out the door.

* * *

At first I didn't know what had happened. Had I been shot or stabbed? Was I about to become one of the often reported crime victims in the Big Apple? No. Wait. I remembered that feeling from my youth. It was nothing more than a snowball thrown with enough force to let me know something had happened. But who…?

As the long winter made a move toward the joy of spring, Holly began to appear again after being often absent from her corner as the snow fell and the ice formed. With a handful of snow she had lobbed the icy missile which hit me in the center of my back. I turned to see Holly, smiling and looking as peevish as a young girl who had just learned the art of snowball throwing.

"That was a good shot," she said. "I hit my target perfectly and I declare myself the winner."

I should have made and thrown a snowball myself but didn't. Instead I walked toward her and hugged her.

"Hello old friend. Yes, it was a perfect shot. Well done."

Looking at her closely I could see a gray hair here and there and a thin line or two around her beautiful eyes still jet black. She wore clothing that was different than usual, more like that worn by a business lady, but not the business she was in.

"Let's get something to eat. I'm famished," she said. After a debate about what kind of dinner we wanted it was decided to go to an area steakhouse which was in walking distance. After entering, being seated, with drinks ordered, she handed me a newspaper article printed recently in a New York newspaper.

The headline immediately grabbed my attention: "Former minister, prostitute earns prestigious teaching position."

"Read it," she said. "I think you will find it interesting."

It was a long article with two photos, one of her alone and one of her in front of a room filled with college-aged students. It told of her days as a minister and as a prostitute and she credited a friend for helping her make the decision to pursue other work such as teaching and a simpler more meaningful lifestyle.

"You are that friend," she said stretching her hand across the table to hold mine. "Remember what I said about the importance of human touch. It is always important. It is always powerful. It is always appropriate."

She explained she had investigated a Position Open Ad in one of the local newspapers. She got more information about it and applied and during her interview was very open about her history, all of it, and was hired by the city university to teach philosophy and religion. "That's right up my alley don't you think?" I could only agree.

"I've retired from the street, but still go to the precinct from time to time as a volunteer. I still live in the same apartment with my pictures and books and a cat. Yes, I got a yellow cat I named Buddha. He sits on top of the books on one of the shelves when he's not sitting on my lap. He is my family now."

"You have to get another cat, Holly, to keep Buddha company when you are not home. You will appreciate their interactions when the three of you are together."

I made the decision to tell her about a change in my life, but not that night.

"Holly, I am traveling to Paris for work for seven to ten days and then I'll be upstate for a week or so and then I will be back here for a few days, not to work, but to see you. Can we get together then?"

"Yes."

We set a date, time, and place and parted company with a hug and kiss. "I'm proud of you Holly. I am so happy with what you have done. Thanks for allowing me to be a part of it."

With that we left the restaurant with her walking to the west and me to the east.

* * *

Paris was Paris, a large, dirty city with constant 24-hour activity, much like Manhattan. There were many historic things to see. Museums, buildings, monuments, but I never had the opportunity to see many of them since I was always working. I had been there before and it was the same this trip with visits, and work, at two different manufacturing facilities with ties to The Company.

Time spent at my home office upstate was spent processing, cataloging, and sending the hundreds of photos I had taken to the advertising department to be used as necessary. I had no say in their use.

What was most in my mind was my planned visit with Holly, a visit I had not been able to forget, because I had news to tell her and to learn how her new profession was going. That date arrived, I was back in the city for a short time, and with great anticipation walked to the pre-arranged restaurant, at the arranged time. She beat me to the table.

There she was, now my best friend, in her suit with a briefcase by her side.

Our conversation began.

* * *

"How are you my friend," I asked.

"Fantastic," she replied. "I had a class tonight and came here from the university. Kids these days," she said. "I have some very good students and a few who will most likely not make it through their time at the university. We talked about Bible history tonight and I offered some of my true thoughts. Only two students left the room. I felt that was not a bad average. Some youngsters have been so brainwashed they can't comprehend there are different ways to think about many things. This at a time when they are supposed to be open minded about things, but that is not always the case."

There was something about Holly that was different. She had never seemed burdened, stressed, or hurried, but there was a difference. She seemed lighter, freer, more like the young girl she once was. She had aged over the years, but it was hard to see. Her beauty had aged, but not withered.

She took a drink of her iced tea and asked, "So, what about you?"

"I have turned in my resignation, Holly. I will make one more trip, but then I am returning to Ohio. I have no real plans once I get home. You were right when you told me you felt I would make a change. It's been a long time coming. I have seen the world through the lens of a camera, but I have not really seen anything. I've been too busy to look. The corporate ladder was such an attractive mistress."

She was silent for a moment. "Yes. I knew you would tire of climbing that ladder and I knew you would make a change, and I think you have made the right decision. I am proud of you for having the courage to make that decision. I am sure it was not easy."

"No, it wasn't. I had a dream job most people would kill to have. I have made friends at my job, and I'll miss them, but I have always thought there was something more important for me to do. Now, I guess I have a lot to explore."

"Yes, you do. Let's eat. I am hungry as a horse in a field with only brown grass to eat. I need some good grain to sustain me."

We ordered. We ate. We had more pleasant conversation, the kind that takes place between friends, and then came the moment I had dreaded after submitting my letter of resignation.

* * *

She gave me her address and phone number and I gave her mine which would be in effect once I arrived back in Ohio. This all took place before the Internet and email so communication was not electronically instant. That was nice. As this is being written I wonder if we haven't lost something important regarding human relations with so much being done for us by the digital world. We are lacking the wonderful feeling created by human contact.

I said, "Someday I might write about you. If I do, what should I call it? She thought a moment and said, "Call it My Favorite Whore." I have honored her title with this piece.

It was time to go. We left the restaurant and it seemed as if there was so much more to talk about, but the time for that had ended.

We parted with a massive hug and a kiss. "Thank you for being a friend when I needed one," she said.

"Likewise," I replied. "I love you Holly. Thank you for your quiet teaching, your trust, your intelligence, your love, and your guidance. I am going to miss you."

"Likewise. I love you too" she said as she began her walk home and mine to the hotel where her street corner was empty.

I cried all the way to the door of the hotel. I had met, potentially for the last time, the best friend I ever had.

* * *

The above story took place more than fifty years ago and few days go by when I don't think of Holly or the lessons she taught me. During that time we have both aged, or I have and hope she has as well. Neither of us ever called or wrote sensing that door had closed, that chapter had come to an end, a good end.

There was never anything physical between us, but there was intimacy based on the issues we discussed. She helped shape my life by knocking off the many rough edges.

Since returning to Ohio my life has been a series of changes just as Holly predicted. I found true meaningful and non-judgmental love, became a vital force in my community, retired, and began to explore the invisible world Holly talked about. She was right.

I learned to not judge people by what they do, to love each and every one of them including myself, and to follow the plan, not one written on paper, but embedded in the soul. I learned to listen, to trust, to believe, and to honor all that had gone before even if I didn't like it.

Sometimes, maybe always, people appear in our lives who have such an influence that time spent with them changes your life. Don't ignore those encounters.

Thank you, Holly Nusbaugh, for teaching me how to love and to trust the plan made for me. Truly, you are My Favorite Whore and I cannot forget you.

THE MAN WHO SAW THINGS

They called me Pig and in the seventh grade and I struggled with the heavy horn case I carried from home every day to school. Inside the case was a shiny new baritone, the instrument the band director felt was right for me. The nickname Pig was appropriate since I was chubby, maybe even fat, but my greatest protector, my mother, called it baby fat and insisted it would go away. It didn't, at least not yet.

The name Pig stuck until my third year in high school when I declared I would enter the ministry. My nickname then became Deacon which stuck until my second year of college when it became the name given to me following my birth. I did not object to being called Deacon, it was better than Pig, and that name stuck through my first college degree but fell away as I began work on an advanced degree.

I loved the wilderness and throughout life spent as much time among the trees and plants as I could. I saw my first "vision" while sitting on the ground with my back against a large oak tree in a section of woods I knew well near my home. I was listening to the noises, some familiar some not, which came from the surrounding forest when a small spot of light was spotted in the plants, some would call weeds, which were near at hand. I was enjoying the smells which only come from the forest and as the spot of light seemed to come nearer its image became clearer as it flew from one plant to the next oblivious to my presence. Or was it?

I thought it must be a dragonfly, but there was something different about it. Its head had human qualities and seemed to be peering around as if observing the various plants and then it became a fuzzy spot of light again and went on its way into the wilderness. I wondered if it might have been a fairy, but quickly changed my mind. No, I thought, it must have been a dragonfly, just a different kind, one I had never seen before. I was still in high school at the time and did not mention seeing the unknown creature to anyone until years later.

Going away to college allowed me the opportunity to explore new forests and I would often study in the calming nature of the trees and plants. It was in these woods that I first noticed the energy of trees and plants and the network of underground energy that fed them both and consequently me. It was here that I picked up a stick shed by a tree and felt its energy as it literally vibrated in my hand. It was also in these woods that I first saw rings of color around the heads of some people, but not all. I was seeing auras but didn't know it at the time. I could look at them and tell who was happy, or sad, or in good or bad health, or those who might soon die. This scared me so I tried to stop seeing such things and was successful to some degree but not totally.

The next 20 years or so were extremely busy academically and professionally but my visions continued to come although not with the power they once had. It wouldn't be long before they came back with a bang.

* * *

There was a small house which sat on about 5 acres of land in the southern part of my home county. It had been occupied by two elderly women for several years, but one died and then the other. I and my wife Nina learned about the history of the small house, which was now empty, got the keys and went for a visit. The front door opened into a room that had served as the bedroom for the two women and in that empty space appeared a bed with an obviously dead woman in it. "This house is holding memories" I said and Nina shook her head in agreement. After a short tour of the remaining three rooms we agreed this was the house for us.

We had spent a lot of time with friends and teachers who had opened our eyes to the meaning of things we both saw or had seen and had educated us about the very real unseen world and we had become true believers.

Our first project increased the size of the structure by adding a larger bedroom as well as a smaller room which could serve as a second bedroom or a small office. The second project was the addition of a large front room and other than the major construction work I did most of the interior work. It was during the construction of the front room I realized the house was holding memories because for the next two or three years my constant companion was the ghost or spirit of the women we had seen on our first visit to the home and she was quite a jokester. We had a ghost.

* * *

After contractors did the framing, put on a roof, installed a floor and windows as well as the outside covering and a ceiling the rest of the work was up to me and a couple of friends. There would be another small bedroom and a loft with stairs leading up to it. In the center of that room sat a 14' step ladder which I needed for the higher work within the room.

When I got home in the afternoons and was ready to work I decided to move the ladder to an area in which I would work next. This was a challenge of sorts because on the very top of that ladder sat a very visible ghost – that of the woman seen when we first entered the house. It appeared she was not yet ready to exit her earthly home and was set on supervising work that was being done to it. She would come and go, but I would talk to her to explain what I was going to do next and explain why. She became an almost constant companion in the home and a welcomed guest.

I was anxious to work one day so I took my keys out of my pocket, laid them somewhere, changed clothes, and got to work. When I went to retrieve my keys that evening, they could not be found even though I looked everywhere, and the sharp-eyed Nina couldn't find them either. This was not a big problem since I always had a second set of the important keys. Two maybe three weeks later the keys were found. I had removed a section of drywall and found them sitting on a piece of 2x4 used as a brace in that wall above an electrical box. Our ghost had been playing games.

I learned to always keep my hammer with me because if I didn't it would vanish to places unknown. One hammer was never accounted for.

And then there was the washing machine which sat in a small laundry room well known to the ghost. Without fail if you would start a load of laundry it would stop mid-cycle. The lid would have been raised and you had to go to that room and close it so it could be raised later in the cycle. This was a game I rather enjoyed playing.

The bedroom had a sliding glass door which was left open on hot summer evenings. There was a screen so there was not a problem leaving the glass part open. One night, late in the night, I felt an animal rubbing against my hand. I petted it believing it was one of our cats, but when getting to its tail I realized it wasn't a cat but an opossum. I shooed it out the door with a broom and made sure the screen was closed and locked. Who or what had opened that screen? I believe our ghost got me again. I went back to sleep and was smiling, maybe laughing.

Eventually the work was finished, the ladder was put back in a garage, and we enjoyed a year or two of comfortable living but then a new living opportunity was found. It seems as if an 80 acre of mostly forest with a couple of barns, a house, a cottage, and a couple of other buildings became available in the opposite end of the county at a reasonable price. We talked about the land, visited it, and liked what we saw, and bought it.

We had not seen our favorite ghost once our south county project was done, but as the furnishings and other items were being removed from the home a little ceremony was held thanking her for being with us and wishing her the best in eternity. Her earthly duty had been completed and now she could enjoy her heavenly reward.

* * *

Moving is never a pleasant project, but once it is done there is a feeling of accomplishment and a sense of moving into a place that will be your forever home. This was in 1993. Nina was an accomplished naturalist, a former nature guide at a reserve, and a student of the unseen world who felt more at peace in the forest or jungle than anywhere else. She was a true practitioner and believer in things unseen, a true student of magical spirituality, and an apostle of spreading true love. I did not have Nina's level of knowledge of the unseen world but did have the experiences of being able to see the unseen world in all its glory. We spent the first few months of life at our new home in the forest exploring every inch of ground in the 80 acres we would take care of to the best of their abilities for the rest of our lives. We had found our forever home and most importantly we had found it together.

Near the back northeast side of the property there was a deep cut in a hillside made by rushing water from one of the land's two streams and I was drawn to that spot and in time constructed a fire ring, which became known as the back fire ring. I could camp there or just sit and listen. But that fire ring had not yet been built. Nina also camped there from time to time to capture and harvest her spiritual needs and to hold ceremony in honor of Mother Earth and all that is within it.

In prehistory the land had been known as the black swamp and with the abundance of wildlife a variety of native peoples would camp at the spot to harvest the meat and herbs they needed as they moved through the area generally heading north toward what is now known as Chillicothe or further north to what is now known as Circleville.

I still saw the small orbs of light usually near the edge of the forest but it was while sitting in that area one fall day I got a glimpse of life as it had been in the 1700 or 1800's. As I looked to the south I watched as a band of about 15 or 20 native people trudged along a path that led to an alluvial pond that sat to the west of where I was sitting. They wore tattered clothing and their faces bore the look of incredible sadness which I will never forget. As the group got nearer the leader, or chief, pointed to a hillside near the pond and walked up a path I had often used. The leader waited until his people had put down the items they had been carrying and began to speak as they moved closer to the spot where he stood.

"We are about out of food," he said. "We have few men to hunt for the food we need and what we can get won't last long. This is as far as we can go. We have fought long and hard, but I believe this is the place where we will die."

It was where the man stood that I built the back fire ring with rocks from the creek below.

I looked out over the small group and noticed it was mostly older men, women, and children. The few younger men were already out hunting for deer or bear or whatever they could find in the wilderness. A camp of sorts was being set up. The people were bone tired and ready for rest. This vision occurred in 1994.

* * *

Fast forward to 2017. I had begun mowing a field, which once held cattle then horses, to make it part of our yard. The field, nearly two acres, is about 100 yards from the location of my 1994 vision. As I was mowing the field a young Native American woman dressed in beautiful ceremonial garb was standing near the edge, just outside of a fence, and was watching me mow. She was smiling and I nodded my head as a way of acknowledging her presence. Then she was gone.

Early in the spring of 2018 that same young smiling women appeared again, and then a week later, again. I acknowledged her presence both times but asked no questions although I had many. She wore the same ceremonial clothing she wore in my 2017 vision.

One week later, on Wednesday, May 3, 2018 I was working in another part of the yard and her image appeared in my mind and I heard the words, "Ask your questions."

"Who are you? I asked.

"I am known as Sun Dancer. I am the daughter of Straight Walker." He apparently was the leader of the tattered group I had seen in 1994.

"Why are you here?"

"First I want to tell you that what you saw was real." She was referring to my vision of 1994.

"Why are you dressed in that beautiful clothing?"

"I wanted to show you how we looked in our happier days. We also want you to know we believe the fire ring you built is a memorial to us and we honor you for that."

She then told me her story. She said her group spent the summers near the Big River (Ohio?) where they fished and hunted. "Today you would call us Shawnees, but that is not what we called ourselves then." As fall approached each year the group would begin its walk to our area of Ohio to hunt for winter supplies and would then continue its walk to another town near another river (Scioto?) to spend the winter with other native groups trading needed items for items they had crafted during the summer. "It was a friendly time. There was no fighting. This we had done for years and years."

She then told of how her group ended up at what is now the property we care for. She said they had started their trip to the north and hunted on the way until they ran into another group that was also hunting and did not want to share the bounty with another group.

"They covered their faces with mud and mixed it with ashes from their fires. Their faces were black and there was a battle and we were defeated. We lost many of our men and boys and were left with only the small group you saw."

She said her group continued its walk, but when it came to the place where I saw them Straight Walker said, "This is as far as we can go."

"We had water, but little or no game so we began dying. Our bones are resting here, but not our spirits." She said at first the dead were buried or at least covered with dirt and stones from the nearby creek, but the last few were left on the ground for the "birds and other creatures that lived here."

I told her I had seen the group from time to time, walking the path that led them to where they would die. I asked why.

"We come here to remember. We build fires in your fire ring but you will notice no difference because they are spirit fires," was all she said.

I thanked her for the information she offered but heard no response.

Later that same day, I was mowing a path into the woods near where the little group had once stood and later died. Something caught my attention ahead of the mower so I stopped. There, near the center of the path, was a large pure white feather so I picked it up and kept it as one of the best and most honored gifts I had ever received.

There is nothing today that lives on our land, or flies above it, which has pure white feathers.

Sometimes in the fall when many leaves have fallen and the brush has turned brown and is low to the ground we can see the trail the native people walked hundreds of years ago from our kitchen window. We see the small group walking again toward the field in which they died so long ago. We always offer a prayer of thanksgiving for their lives and for the richness their story adds to the place we call home.

LIFE AT THE TOP OF THE HILL

When my wife and I lived in the south end of our county we lived on a piece of sloping property which ended in a flat, level spot where our home had been built directly across the road from an elementary school. The upward slope continued for a mile or so and on top of that hill stood a home occupied by Clark and Emelia Winters. They had been involved in the theatre in New York but had moved to Ohio to begin work at a theatre in Cincinnati. He was a well thought of costume designer and artist and she was a stage manager. After searching for property they bought land at the top of the hill and began a variety of building projects including a home.

For a time their wedding had been a south county legend, an event few if any from that area had ever seen. Traffic on the narrow country roads came to a standstill as many as 100 vehicles lined the roads with no place else to park. When it came time for the ceremony a large contingent of visitors including some entertainment elite carried flags and banners up the hill to the spot chosen for the event. It was on that spot they built their home. They first built a barn in which they lived while other projects took place, then another barn to house the goats they raised and sold, and then the house.

Clark was busy with his theatre duties in Cincinnati and Emilia worked as a server at a local eatery and as they watched the fish in a small pond swim about as fish do, the goats happily munching away at the feed they were given, and the bamboo growing around the pond they had created as well as the plants growing in a greenhouse they had attached to the house they had achieved their dream, or at least most of it. We first met Emilia when she worked at a local restaurant and she was very good at what she was doing but it was obvious she was not locally born or raised. Her accent wasn't the same as ours and her manner was that of someone who had been raised in a different lifestyle than we had, but she was polite, efficient, and if mistakes were made on an order the fault was not hers.

Life was good and it was for a while.

* * *

Early one evening a knock came at our front door. It was Clark and Emelia and they came to visit and to ask a question. After brief chit-chat Emelia said they had read my story about the restaurant closing so I knew she was without a job. Clark was doing most of his work from home making only an occasional trip to Cincinnati and they wondered if there were any openings at the newspaper I owned especially for a reporter. After discussion and an explanation of what I could pay they were both hired, Emelia as a reporter and Clark to assist with paper delivery one time each week. Sometimes you just know when hiring someone is the right thing to do.

Having additional personnel worked well for quite some time until Emelia announced one morning that Clark had become ill and the diagnosis was cancer. He would work as long as he could, but no one knew how long that might be. The news affected us all. We had become a close-knit family and to have a member sick took a toll on each person in the office.

Clark had surgery and the doctor felt he had eliminated all the cancer, but as time went on it became obvious he was losing ground and more and more Emelia became a caregiver and her work as a reporter became less and less. That was understood even encouraged. In life there are things that are more important than being at work.

This all happened before the age of the cell phone, texting, and other marvelous advances made in communication so we stayed close to our home phone. My wife and I took turns relieving Emelia because being the caretaker of a person you love is a daunting, exhausting task, but Emelia was with him the majority of time.

One evening the anticipated call came. Emelia felt Clark had a very short time to live. Could we come up to sit with her? We were there in minutes.

We sat around the bed each of us watching the clock after each breath. Then the last breath was drawn.

The funeral home had advance notice of the possibility of Clark passing and was at the hill top home not long after the final call was made. I helped take his body out of the home and load it into the hearse. Hugs were offered all around and for the first time in years Emelia was alone in the home she and Clark had built on the top of the hill. I could only imagine what she was feeling and thinking.

That chapter of life had closed.

* * *

When Emilia returned to work after Clark's passing she had changed in a most positive way. It seemed as if she was in the process of blossoming like a bud on a rose bush. She was always smart, organized, and efficient, but now those things were enhanced and she was becoming her own person, thinking for herself, and that had a positive effect on everything she did. Her talents were blooming.

Emelia was not a trained journalist but had a sense of what was important and what was not and wrote stories from another part of our county which hadn't been ignored but wasn't covered to the depth I preferred. She developed her own style of writing which was a bit folksy but those who read the paper seemed to love it. I did some editing to make it fit the newspaper mold, but not much. Her articles were always timely and accurate and sometimes dealt with issues the paper would not cover but which were appropriate. She more or less set her own schedule and covered what she thought best and I usually agreed.

She worked part-time at the newspaper and then at her other job as director of an arts organization which she and Clark had started, or resurrected, in the county and was in the process of renovating an old building which would be used as a theatre and an art gallery and classes would be offered to budding artists from the area. They had already started an annual arts festival which was very popular and was something new and different in the county. At first art work was displayed outdoors in large tents and then in a large indoor space which eliminated the need to fret about the whims of Mother Nature. Her life was full and she always had a smile on her face. She would hum or whistle while she worked.

When she learned that another employee would be leaving she and I talked about the sale of the paper and she agreed to move to a new office in a different town with me and to continue to work as usual and all was fine once again. "This will work out just fine," she told me and it did. We both were in a very different work situation with coverage areas increased and the new version of the Old Hometown Paper now published twice each week as opposed to just one time. There was a new larger staff was in place in order to produce a good local newspaper, but for me the thrill of publishing was gone. I played along as did Emilia she probably more so than me.

* * *

The perfect life is for married couples to grow old together and although Emilia and I were not married we had a strong friendship which remains solid today. While working together we had lunch together at least once each week and we both looked forward to that special time.

She retired several years before I made that life-changing move but we still got together from time to time usually to eat lunch and for updates on life in general. At some point in time we both ended up serving on the same board so had time to talk and reminisce. But there is far more to her story than mine. She was not done making positive changes in the community she had come to love.

* * *

After her retirement Emilia now had time to devote entirely to the restoration and eventual use of the arts center she, and others, had been working on for several years. She had made a number of influential friends, many in government, who supported her cause and worked with her to get various grants with each helping to complete another phase of renovation.

Ultimately the project was completed with art shows being held and then stage performances and eventually old movies. While she stayed at the theatre for a time her dream - and Clark's – had been realized. It was time to really retire.

"I am bone tired," she told me at her retirement party.

While she remained active in the community and took care of business where she could she also faced health issues but worked through them as they arose.

In her life this woman from New York had added depth and expertise to a local newspaper and then to a newer version of the same paper, founded an arts festival, and saw an old and tattered building turned into a modern state of the arts facility.

That's not a bad resume for a transplanted New Yorker who came to love the community that had loved and adopted her.

CHILDHOOD FRIENDS

Once you reach a certain point in an advancing life, childhood memories seem to have become a part of who you are. Often forgotten during a busy professional life, they have remained filed away in a portion of the brain not to surface again until time is available to sit quietly immersed in memory. Suddenly the old issues and memories are there like potatoes rolling off a potato cart and they take on an importance not earlier imagined. Some of those concern people who were important in an earlier life, and maybe now, and they are written here in an abbreviated form.

Billy Woodgear

Billy and I lived just a block from each other, walked to school together every day, and were both learning to play musical instruments at the same time. His father was the minister of one of the town's churches and had a college degree and had attended seminary. He was a very bright man or so it seemed to me. His mother was a stay-at-home mom at a time when that was the norm. She was quite nurturing even to a kid who lived just down the street. I never heard a voice raised in that home.

Billy was a quiet boy, quite the opposite from me, but perhaps his home life dictated his behavior which was, at that age, top notch which was how most kids were back in the 1950's.

When I would say or do something Billy felt was wrong he would say, "Well, ain't that just a corn husk." When asked what that meant he would say he didn't know. It was something his dad often said.

Sitting in their living room one afternoon following school Billy and I were playing a board game and I made a move which stopped Billy's progress in its tracks. As a result he said, "Well, ain't that just a corn husk."

His dad, sitting in his chair reading the local paper, looked at us past the paper and smiled. "What's that mean?" I asked.

Putting the paper aside his dad thought for a moment and asked, "Have you ever had corn on the cob?" I said I had. He followed by asking, "What happened before you ate the corn?" I explained the process my mother used in pulling off the husk and cleaning off the pesky hairs which appeared next to the cob of corn.

"What did your mother do with the husks," he asked. I said she threw them away.

In a moment, he said that is what most people do. "Corn husks are important," he said. "They protect the corn when it is growing, but you can't eat it so it gets thrown away after exposing that wonderful corn on the cob." After another thoughtful pause he said, "It's a lot like life. Sometimes you must throw away the bad things that happen before you can enjoy the good that lies inside. So when you think something is wrong or out of line you can discard it by saying well, ain't that just a corn husk and it is gone. Tossed away. Do you understand now?"

I said I thought I did and I must have because I remember that lesson to this day and have followed the good pastor's advice.

Billy's father accepted the call to another church before we made it to high school and I did not see him again, but childhood friends and the memories made with them remain for a very long time.

Tomi Applecraft

Tomi was one of two girls in the Applecraft home. The other girl was Cindi and was a couple of years older so was passed the age when she was interested in a boy my age. But Tomi was and we spent countless hours together in a treehouse I had built with the help of others and hours walking in a cemetery near our homes. We just talked, never anything more. What brought us together was her love of rockets.

As a kid I always had a chemistry lab and after time I learned to make gunpowder and then learned how to load a can with it, light it and stand back. Those early rockets never went very far and now and then would fall to the ground with a mighty explosion. I had not yet learned how to make them fly straight, but I shared the gunpower formula with Tomi and she, having a different kind of mind or thought process, experimented and developed a better formula and then thought of putting fins on the cans to make them fly straighter.

Then we combined our skills and made a launching ramp and developed a fuse instead of sticking a match into a hole at the bottom of the can. Our first rocket was small but flew maybe 50 yards before burning out and falling to the ground and it went almost straight. Our next rocket was larger, had larger fins, and flew farther and landed in a grassy area maybe 75 yards from my home, the site of the wooden launching pad.

Tomi suggested we take our third rocket, the largest so far, to an area where it had more room to fly so we took our loaded rocket and launching pad to an undeveloped area of the cemetery, aimed the rocket so it would fly over a slight hill, and land in an area where we might be able to find it to be used again in another flight. But something went wrong.

After lighting the fuse the rocket seemed to be flying straight and was near the slight rise but then made a sharp turn to the left and headed straight for an old unused barn where it exploded setting the structure on fire. We really didn't know what to do so I threw the launching pad into the woods and started to slowly walk home. By the time we got to her house we could hear a firetruck coming. By the time I got home I watched as the truck passed our house and headed up the hill toward the cemetery.

　　We never made another rocket.

SISTER MARY AGNES COOPER

Walking into the Absolute Truth of Jesus Christ Tabernacle was like walking into a place unknown to me. Dim lights, the taped rhythm of a bass guitar coming quietly from two large speakers at the front of the church, a stage filled with musical instruments including one of the largest drum sets I had ever seen, what appeared to be a large bathtub covered with a plastic cover, about 200 seats each covered by a plush red pad, and stage lights which had not yet been turned on.

I had retired from the hum-drum and challenging life of a newspaper owner/editor so did not arrive at the tabernacle to do a story, but to honor the invitation of a friend who was a member of the congregation to attend. I did so with a certain level of trepidation.

Near the stage was an elderly woman, later identified to me as Sister Mary Agnes Cooper, who was kneeling with tears rolling down her cheeks and right arm raised with a finger pointing to a picture of a person I assumed was Jesus. The picture seemed to have been painted on black velvet and showed the image of a man with flowing black hair, blue eyes, and pale skin, nothing at all like the presumed Jesus, a dark skinned Jew, would appear. Put a guitar in the hands of the man shown and he would appear to be a player in a rock and roll band or a young Elvis.

Bishop Emerson Peoples entered, introduced himself as pastor of the church, and we sat down in the back pew to talk. I introduced myself and said I was there as a guest invited by Mary Barbee who had once worked for me. "Yes, I know Sister Mary quite well," Peoples said. "She was one of our earliest members and one of our most loyal."

I pointed to the woman kneeling in front, he identified her, and said she often came to the church prior to the Wednesday night service to pray to Jesus and to ask forgiveness for the sins she is sure she had committed. "She is terrified about going to Hell," Peoples said. "I tell her she has been born again so her sins are forgiven, but she continues to come and if that gives her peace of mind I can't see anything wrong with that."

I said the Pope had recently told his people that Hell did not exist, an idea that had earlier been stated by a retired bishop of the Catholic Church in a televised interview. Hell, he said, had been used by the church as a way of controlling its people which induced fear and that was unnecessary.

"Yes, I heard something about that," Peoples said, "but we believe in the Bible and not what some Catholic says." He added, "If we can't make our people live in fear of Hell we can't inspire them to live Christian lives. If they live the way good Christians should they do not have to fear Hell. The Pope does not run this church. I do."

He went on. "We are Bible believers, every word of it, because it is the truth. Most churches don't believe like that anymore so we feel we are the one true church. If you want to enjoy the golden streets of Heaven, you will worship with us." It would have been foolish of me to ask where golden streets were promised in the Bible so I did not push that question or several others I had formulated in my mind. That was not the purpose of my visit.

I did ask about the various interpretations of the Bible. "Every author does a rewrite every now and then," he said. "Even God. So when He feels a new interpretation is needed He does a rewrite. You can believe me when I say God's hand was in every interpretation of that great book."

I asked, "What about the books that were left out?"

"That was part of the rewrite. God did it and if He did it that's fine with me."

The Bishop said, "When we started here about a year ago we had 75 people come to our service. Now every seat is filled and we are talking about adding an addition to hold at least 200 more. We have been blessed with a very generous group of believers and we will build the addition and pay for it without having to borrow money. Many blessings have come our way. That says to me that we are doing the right things here."

I then asked about the idea that Jesus is God. "Yep, that's right because it says so in the Bible. You read it and you will see for yourself."

I asked where he had studied to become a pastor. "I didn't," was his reply. "I grew up in a home with a mother and father who were believers in the Bible and what it said. We didn't question a single word and I still don't. When I was still in high school I got the call to preach. It came out of the blue but was clear as a bell. So I helped in one of our area churches, learned how to pronounce the words, and learned how important a good gospel band was. I preached a couple of times at that church, but my beliefs were stronger than theirs so I began to search for my own church."

After a few moments he continued. "I found this building which had belonged to a group of Pentecostals, but they had disbanded and I borrowed money from my parents to buy it. I paid them back less than a year after I bought it."

"How did you get the title of Bishop," I asked. "Our congregation gave me that honor," he replied. "We don't belong to any group other than ourselves. Other churches in the area have pastors who are called Bishop, so why shouldn't we?" I could not answer that without getting into an argument, so I didn't try.

"So," I asked, "what are your future plans?"

"Well, I told you about our expansion plans. That project will start very soon. Then, depending on how everything goes, we will expand again. I am working on buying the next two lots to make way for a lot of growth. Then we will start a school for our young people so they don't have to deal with the problems in public schools and will be prepared to continue our work when I am gone. Past that I can't tell. We will have to see what happens, but I can tell you this: We will always be Bible believers. What that book says is the truth, every word of it, and I don't care what someone from another church says or does, we will not change. If you want to go to Heaven you better be attending this church."

After a moment of thought he said, "We believe Jesus is going to come again and we feel we will be the first to know it right here in this church. When the ceiling opens up and a big glow comes in we will see Jesus with arms outstretched floating down to the floor. I think he will land right there," he said pointing to an open area near the pulpit.

"When that happens, we will join Him and follow Him to Heaven where we will enjoy the benefits of living good Christian lives. I have no doubt about it at all. That's how it will happen, and it will happen here."

People started arriving at the church, lots of them, so I thanked Bishop Peoples for his time and took a seat in the back row of the church. The music began and some people began to dance, others knelt in prayer, and some just sat quietly as if in prayer many holding Bibles.

The service opened with the band playing a kick-ass Christian song and singers, some with great voices, sang the praises of their God, Jesus. It brought back memories of one of the James Brown concerts

I had attended earlier in my life. The juices were certainly beginning to flow.

When I left the church, shortly after Bishop Peoples began to offer his message in a booming voice that I am sure could be heard two streets away, Sister Mary Agnes was still kneeling near the stage, tears were still running down her face as she sought something she believed in and would until her very last breath, but she did not seem to feel better, or more assured, about anything at all.

* * *

Sister Mary Agnes had a secret.

After attending part of the service earlier in the week I mentioned my visit to the church to a friend who asked if Mrs. Cooper had been there. I replied she had been, but I didn't speak with her since she seemed to be consumed by prayer. "That sounds like her," he said. "One of these days you should talk with her. She has an interesting story to tell, but she won't tell you much unless you can get her to trust you. I knew her quite well a lot of years ago but that's all I am going to say. The rest you will have to learn on your own."

Being recently retired with a small amount of the juice of newspapering still in my blood it didn't take me long to find Mary Agnes Cooper in our small town. In fact, one visit to the police station gave me all the information I needed.

She lived in a small white house in the south end of town near where a school once stood. There was nothing fancy about the home, but the yard was neat and a few colorful flowers were blooming along the front and sides of a porch. The house itself could have used a coat of paint, but it was not deteriorated as much as some in the neighborhood. I knocked on the door.

I noticed a curtain in the front door got pushed to the side as Mrs. Cooper looked me over and then opened the door. I introduced myself and was invited in. She pointed to a chair I was to sit in and asked if I wanted something to drink which I declined. She was elderly, maybe in her 80's, and wore a comfortable house dress with large, brightly colored flowers printed on the fabric and on her feet were white tennis shoes.

"I saw you in church the other night," she said. "Are you thinking of joining us or where you just visiting Bishop Peoples? I explained I had been invited to the service and was just visiting. I said a friend of mine had suggested I talk with her because he felt she had an interesting story to tell.

"What was your friend's name," she asked. "Bill Riley" I replied. "Oh yes. Billy Riley. I knew him back in the day and he was a good friend at that time. He's been quite successful you know. He sells a lot of homes in town. In fact, he sold me this house many years ago and then when it needed painted he found a painter for me. It's about time to have it painted again."

Mary Agnes did not seem like the same person I had seen in church. She was perky, even animated at times, was not crying and had a sparkle in her eyes that reminded me of my grandmother when she was a young woman. "Are you the man who owned a newspaper here some time ago?" I said I was. "Are you going to write something about me?" I said I had not planned to and explained I just found people interesting and was no longer connected to the newspaper.

"What do you want to know?" she asked. "I don't have many visitors these days." After a moment she said, "Stay there. I am going to get us some iced tea and then we'll talk." I didn't have to say a word for the next hour or so.

* * *

"My mother, father and I moved here when I was 13 or 14. Dad was an engineer and worked for a company that manufactured equipment for the coal business. Eventually he died, and then mom and I were all alone so I took a job as a seamstress at a factory that made clothing for men. I worked there until it closed and I saved every penny I could," she said taking a drink of iced tea. "Then I got married."

"I didn't realize you were married," I said.

"Well, it didn't last long only three months, but it was a marriage. I had been raised to be an independent, free-thinking woman and Johnny, well he was the kind of man you find here. He was the boss and called all the shots and made all the decisions. He seemed to feel I was his property. We were together only a short time and my independent streak ended that marriage. Really, the only thing I enjoyed was the sex." She took a rather long sip of iced tea and said, "Can I tell you some really private things?"

"Sure. If you are comfortable telling me those things."

"You will not tell?"

"My lips are sealed."

"After my marriage ended, I missed the closeness, the intimacy. I didn't miss my husband, but I did miss the time we spent alone in the bedroom and in other places. There was a man who worked in a local business and I always found him interesting so we began to talk and eventually….well you know what happened. We spent time together for several months, but he was married and his guilt ended that relationship, but I had experienced the taste of something new and wanted more."

From there she talked about different relationships. There were weekends spent in distant cities, a number of meetings with men in church parking lots during Wednesday night services, a couple of cruises to the Caribbean, her favorite country road parking spots in the local area, the back row at the drive in movie, and more. The stories went on and on. I felt like a priest during confession.

"Do you think I was a tramp" she asked. "No…I think you were a woman with needs and you met them in your own way. I think you lived a life many women would want and maybe even admire."

As we were finishing our third glass of iced tea I asked why she had been kneeling, praying, and crying at church that evening.

"I met Bishop Peoples and liked him but not in the way I once liked men. He seemed sincere and decent and he invited me to church. I started going and during that time he taught me about God and Jesus and his own beliefs. He said I should fear God because He would decide if I would go to Heaven with its streets of gold after I die or to the eternal fire of Hell. I thought about what he said and then thought about my life and realized I was a sinner, that God would not think kindly about a woman like me, a woman who had done the things I had done, and would send me to Hell. I got scared so I began to pray, and pray, and pray as a way of releasing the debt I myself had earned. Bishop Peoples said Jesus forgave me of all my sins, but I don't see how that can happen."

I said I wasn't a preacher or a theologian or a student of the Bible, but I had my beliefs and asked if she was interested in hearing them. She said she was.

I told her I saw God as a loving creator who would not judge us and send us to a fiery forever. I said I did not believe in Heaven or Hell because I felt they were tools used by the church to capture us and some of our money for its own use. I told her I believed Jesus was the son of God, but she was also, and me, and everyone who had life. I said I believed we all have a spark of God within us. Jesus, I said, was a great teacher but I did not see him as anything else. The only person who could forgive her of what she saw as sin was her.

She stared at me for a moment and said, "I've never thought of those things before. You have given me a different perspective to consider. Thank you."

I told her she and Bishop Peoples and those in his church will believe as they choose to believe, and I wouldn't attempt to change those beliefs, but every coin has two sides and each needs to be considered.

When we parted company she thanked me for talking with her and I thanked her for telling me her story. She kissed me on the cheek.

* * *

Six months or so after my visit I read that Mary Agnes Cooper had died with visitation and services being held a couple days later. I visited the funeral home more out of curiosity than anything else and Mary Agnes looked spectacular. She was no longer crying but had a slight smile on her face, sort of like the Mona Lisa, and held a small wooden cross in her hands. She had no family so attendance was sparse.

I didn't stay for the service leaving shortly after my visit at the casket. I left thankful that her fear-laden journey was over and that she was now in a very different place and I hoped the smile on her face meant she was happy with her new life which had moved from the physical to the spiritual.

A TIME OF BLOOD, GUTS, AND DEATH

Caving into pressure from our south county neighbors and members of a small township fire department my wife and I took our training and became firefighters in that department. I would not call myself an expert in fighting fire, but due to a small, but engaged, membership I became chief in a short time. There was one truck which had major mechanical issues such as no brakes and a pump that worked only when it decided to do its job. I was thankful that some members were able to bring the truck up to working status. I am not a mechanic. There is a time in life when becoming involved in public service is important. For me firefighting was that opportunity.

I owned a newspaper in a town not too far away and was busy. My wife was also busy as a social worker in several different organizations but had settled into an agency job. Still, there we were, me as chief in a department with almost no working firefighting equipment and she as a valued and knowledgeable firefighter. Really, she should have been chief, not me.

The town in which I worked had a bigger fire department with several trucks and a membership that eclipsed that of our south county department. As fate would have it, the mayor of that town checked the legal ramifications and named me to that department as a firefighter. I became busier.

Thank God for firefighters and all emergency response personnel who protect the property and lives of those they serve. A bond is created between all firefighters who run into, not away from, burning structures and from grizzly accidents which give the members an opportunity to see things no one should have to see.

Both departments on which I served had their share of fires and accidents. In some incidents a structure or a life was lost. In others one or both were saved. On balance I felt the work was important and necessary and seemed to be appreciated by those served. At least almost all fire levies, when placed on a ballot, are approved by voters. It was community service since I never was paid for the work I provided, at least not enough to pay for the work clothing I lost doing what firefighters do. It was not about the money. It was about being of service to others when they needed it.

Back then PTSD was not mentioned and not understood, thus not treated, and all emergency response workers experience it and it goes untreated and remains in the minds of those who experience it. You did the best work you could do and absorbed what you had experienced. Some things never leave your mind and a few of them are what the coming words describe.

* * *

X - Have you seen, or heard, a man burning to death? I have. Two large trucks collided and one of them caught fire. Due to the damage caused by the collision the man in the burning truck could not get out of his vehicle and was begging for help but we could not get close enough to him due to the flames to assist. No matter how much water was put on the burning cab of the truck the fire would not be suppressed and before our eyes the man burned to death. Once his screaming stopped we could only watch as his body burned.

X - On a snowy and cold morning we were called to an accident on a rural country road. A woman who was looking at a deer on the side of the road had driven left of center and met a snowplow that was coming in the opposite direction. Damage to her vehicle was great and she sat in the front seat. Law enforcement personnel had gotten to the scene a few minutes before we arrived and had gotten her door opened but could not get her out of the vehicle. She slumped in her seat and blood dripped from her left hand, fell on the ground, and froze like a stalactite in a cave. We had to cut the roof off of the car to get her out and when we did we found two young boys in the back seat dressed for school with book bags and papers scattered everywhere. We did not know they were there and both were dead. One of the men on the other side of the car dropped the roof and vomited. I stood frozen not willing to believe what we were seeing. Finally the bodies were removed and we put our gear away and headed back to the station. I have often wondered about the husband and father when he heard the news. And there was the snowplow driver. I'd be willing to bet he has never forgotten that crash which was not his fault.

X - Then there was the elderly couple whose vehicle was struck in the side as they were turning to cross lanes at an intersection. We had to use pneumatic equipment to get the wife's door open and then two, maybe three, of us removed her and carefully carried her to a helicopter which had been called and was waiting near the crash. I will never forget the look of absolute fear on her face as we carried her to the helicopter and medical personnel got her into the chopper. The helicopter got on the way heading north but then made a quick turn to the south. We knew what that meant. She had either died or was so badly injured she was being taken to a closer hospital. We later learned she had died, but her husband survived despite serious injuries.

X - A call came to the department from a neighboring county requesting we respond to a one person fatal accident on a distant rural road to assist in removing the victim from his vehicle. When we arrived the driver had already been pronounced dead and since the crash had occurred near his home a number of neighbors and others who knew him had gathered at the scene. The problem was that he, for some reason, had driven off the right side of the road and a tree limb had gone through the windshield, entered his forehead, and exited through the back of his skull. Emergency responders are used to seeing brain matter at accident scenes, but if anyone at the scene had not seen that material there was plenty to be observed. How do you remove such a victim from a vehicle? Ultimately it was decided that we would cut the tree limb off in front of and behind his skull and that is how he went to the funeral home.

X - There is a kind of humor at accident scenes but that humor is often not seen until months later. A car loaded with young adults had been t-boned on an area four lane road and at least one, maybe two, passengers had been ejected and were dead. EMS personnel were already on scene when we arrived, the two dead had been sheeted, but four were on the ground being cared for. I am not and was not an EMT, but one of the paramedics told me to get some 4x4's (gauze pads) from one of the squad units and cut the jeans off of one of the young ladies who had a deep wound in her left thigh. He would join me as soon as he worked with those who had more serious injuries. The young woman was conscious and talked to me as I used a very sharp pocket knife to remove her bloody jeans. I apologized for doing what I had to do and she realized why it had to be done. I did notice she was wearing white panties with a pattern of large red hearts on them.

Fast forward about six months. I was shopping at our local Walmart one afternoon and a young woman approached me, said she thought she recognized me, and asked if I had cut the pants off a woman who had been in a vehicle crash. I said I had and she replied she was the young woman who had worn panties with large red hearts on them and that she was fine even if she had a large scar on her left thing. She thanked me for helping her that day. I guess that can be thought of as a success story, or at least one with a happy ending.

Above are just a few of the incidents I remember. But I remember all of them and several more and am haunted by some of them especially the two young boys we did not know were in the car until we cut the roof off.

After several years of service I retired from the fire service for a variety of reasons but have a lot of good memories from those years, but still struggle with a few that for some reason simply refuse to go away.

KIDS I REMEMBER

Brittany Hughes, while a senior at Wellsboro High School, was elected as the homecoming queen. It was an honor well deserved.

At almost six feet in height she was not at all athletic, but was one of the most beautiful girls in the school. With perfectly curled and flowing strawberry blond hair, clear and sharp deep blue eyes, makeup that could be the work of a makeup artist, and a body which was perfectly formed much like the statues of ancient goddesses she was a sight to be seen. Nothing in the body of Ms. Hughes was imperfect and she was noticed by her male and female classmates as well as members of the local community.

She had only one drawback: she was dumb as a brick and was lucky to make it through high school. Her beauty, though, made it clear she had a long and hopefully happy life ahead of her. In many cases beauty trumps brains.

Her parents were solid working class people who produced only Brittany. Her father, known as Hank, went to work in a local gas station while still in high school and eventually became the owner of the station and had the reputation of being the town's best automobile mechanic. Her mother, Florence, known predictably as Flo, worked as a clerk in one of the town's clothing stores and made a career of it until the store closed due to a loss of clientele following the arrival of a local big box store. For a while she worked in the new, big store, but not for long feeling the sense of the local community had been lost. She and Hank loved their little community of 6,000 nestled in the rolling hills of Southeast Ohio.

Brandon Clark, one of Brittany's classmates, was to young manhood just what Brittany was to young womanhood. He was captain and quarterback of the football team, was thin, tall, and fit and could have been a model for an ancient sculptor. He was quarterback smart, was a good student, and ended his high school years as 14th in his class of 103. His career in high school football meant he would be honored for the rest of his life by those who felt such things were important in his hometown. His hopes of a collegiate career in football were dashed by the team's 3-7 season. So much pressure was placed on winning that if you, or your team did not, the future was less bright.

His parents were good workers with his father, Bill, a former football star, working in a manufacturing facility and within a few years became a supervisor, then took a position in the business office and became one of those who ran the company. Brandon's mother, Betty, became a bookkeeper in a large company and ultimately became the head of that department. They had a daughter, Cecelia, who married just after high school and left town with her husband for the bright lights and good jobs in a city in the center of the state. They did not come home often.

With their family histories it only made sense that Brittany and Brandon had too much in common to not get together as a couple during their senior year which they did.

Claudia Capanelli, a student who came to the school as a junior, was not at all pretty. In fact she was rather plain, always had her face stuck in a book of some sort, kept to herself, did not join clubs, and had few good friends, only those who seemed to mirror her values, mostly girls who could be classified as geeks as Claudia had been. She was a little chubby, not grossly so, but enough that she would not have been chosen as a model for any sculptor. Her hair was always unruly, never really fixed, and she did not own any makeup and usually wore loose fitting and comfortable clothing, often mismatched when it came to color. She didn't seem to care. She was, however, very smart and became the top graduating student in her class and her speech during graduation ceremonies focused on how an outsider can be adopted as one of the city's own. "You are a warm and welcoming community putting your arms around a girl who came here to live and who loves our schools and town as much as she possibly could," she told the crowd. "I could not choose a better town in which to live."

She and her mother, Sylvia, moved to the city after the death of Sylvia's husband and Claudia's father, Charles. Sylvia took one of the top leadership roles in the same manufacturing facility in which Bill Clark worked. Since they worked in the same office they knew each other, but it was a business relationship and nothing more. In a small town everyone knows everyone even in the chaotic environment of a large manufacturing facility.

After high school Brandon attended a community college and became an LPN. After a year or so he went back to college, became an RN, and after several years of work in that field became a physical therapist. He was familiar with the injuries he suffered in football and wanted to help those who might be suffering with the same sort of injuries.

During his early years in college he and Brittany married and had the first of their three beautiful children, a son named William Clark. They called him Hank. Brittany was a stay-at-home mom and did a good job of it. She became a good cook and kept a happy, clean and well organized household. They had two more children, a daughter named Chloe and another son named Franklin. They were considered pillars of their community and attended one of the many churches in the community where Brittany helped with Bible School, an annual event always held not long after graduation.

When Claudia left town for college, she was not often seen in the community. For her, everything involved books, more books, and lots of study. The few friends she made in high school drifted away following marriage, a move away from the city, or other reasons which stole young people away from the town in which they wanted to stay but couldn't due to limited employment opportunities.

Mother Sylvia quickly became a vital part of the community. She joined the major clubs, took part in every community event, made good, lifetime friends, and purchased a different home, a large brick house just south of the city, and put down deep roots. When offered an opportunity to take a better position at a larger plant she turned it down. She had found her home and intended to stay and did until her retirement years later. At that point she remained involved in the community, even more so, and became known for the parties she held every so often in which people from all levels of the community were invited. She was also known for her financial assistance to the city she had loved for years.

When Claudia returned years later she did so as a medical doctor, a surgeon with a growing positive reputation, at a hospital about 50 miles from town. She set down her roots in that town and never married. She was still the girl with her nose stuck in a book, still slightly chubby, but it was said she had magic in her hands. She and her old classmate Brandon Clark spoke often as she sent some of her patients to him for post-surgical work. Claudia always asked about Brittany during their conversations.

* * *

As is the case in much of our society, high schools hold important reunion events each year with classes honored at different levels of longevity. At the 20 year level, the class which prepared Brittany, Brandon, and Claudia for life after high school met in the cafetorium of one of the school's new buildings. Since Claudia, Brandon, and Brittany had stayed in touch they sat together at a table set for six.

Before they took their seats, those who had been jocks in high school stood in a group, drinks in their hands, and told stories about different games and selected plays most greatly exaggerated. While each was leading solid, respectable, and community-oriented lives they were still jocks at heart.

The girls who had been cheerleaders or majorettes sat at a table and loudly giggled as they remembered their younger days and activities. Most had married, had children, and had become good community members. They were more than just a group of giggling women, but at reunions memories of an older life surfaced. The cliques that had formed in high school still existed which is why some former students avoided the reunion event as they would the plague. The high school experience was not the best time of the lives for some.

"You have certainly made a name for yourself," Brittany said to Claudia.

"Maybe," Claudia replied. "But look at what you and Brandon have accomplished. You have three fine children, some in school, some working, all three productive citizens and Brandon, well Brandon and I have worked together for several years now. I'd say you two have a lot for which you can be proud."

"Yes," said Brittany. "But you have earned a great reputation as a surgeon and have made a lot of money."

"It's not about money, Brittany. We have all been successful, just in different ways. I really envy you guys. You have everything I don't. I fell in love with medicine and you two fell in love with each other and with your children. There are days I would give up what I do to know that feeling. On the score card of life you guys are the winners."

She thought a moment and said, "I love my patients, each and every one of them, and I do my best to help them as much as I can. But it's not the kind of love I can take home and cuddle with, it's not the kind of love that creates new lives to shape and love and care for. I can't relate to that kind of love because I've never had it and never will. Don't get me wrong. I love what I am doing and will do, but still I envy you guys. I always have and always will. You have added good lives to the world, each with bits and pieces of each of you in them and I hope you understand what a joyful world you have helped create."

"And, because of what you have done, I love each of you."

Before Brandon or Brittany could reply, Claudia's phone rang. "Really? Okay, I'll be there in an hour."

"I have to go," Claudia said. "This is the downside of medicine. I have a patient in the ER who has been in an accident, has more broken bones than anyone has been able to count, and needs surgery as soon as possible."

She got up, put on her coat, and started to leave, but turned around. "Remember what I said Brittany. You guys are the winners. Don't ever forget that." And she was gone.

HEAD IN A BOX

It is not common for two grown men to start a letter writing practice, but that's what happened in the early 1980's and continued until midway through 2019 when the letters abruptly stopped coming with no explanation. Almost 40 years of enlightening ideas and comments, each greatly anticipated and appreciated, each bringing another peek into the persona of the writer, each mentioning thoughts about this or that, and each showing a side of each that most people never saw. We were two very different individuals, he the scholar who took want he believed from his books and me, the spiritually centered artist who formed his beliefs from direct experience and a life lived according to the rules of and in nature.

We were like oil and water but we did mix, at least on paper, each explaining to the other what we believed, how, and why with each learning from the other and then possibly changing our beliefs based on the ramblings of the other. We only met face-to-face two times, once when I was visiting the school in which he taught and later unexpectedly in a restaurant my wife and I visited for an evening meal.

Yet, we became friends through the letters we wrote and then one day the letters stopped. I wrote the last one and received no more letters from him after that. After nearly forty years the exercise was over.

* * *

We grew to adulthood in the same small town, didn't know each other and went in similar directions, but with different consequences. Somewhere in the town an invisible line existed and although invisible there was a definite difference in attitude and the way people thought. Somewhere south of the old high school, near the football stadium, something changed. The two resulting areas became the South End and the North End.

The South End became home to a class of people who for some unknown reason became the lower class at least in how they thought or how people thought about them. There was a school there and the students were just as bright as those from the North End, but the attitude was different and changed the students for the rest of their lives. Many in that area were the downtrodden, the working poor, the down and out, those who stayed in town for the rest of their lives and created families there, and a short list of business people. Most of them were, however, good, hardworking people. They were born in a section of town that had an invisible shadow hanging above it, a shadow that shaped far too many lives.

That is where Bill was born and raised.

The North End was where the seat of local government could be found and where the supposedly upper class lived. This is where the business owners lived, the professional people, and those who went on to college to live productive lives and to create businesses for the benefit of all. This is not to say there were not downtrodden in the North End because there were, just not as many. The attitude was definitely different and you could feel it if you drove, or walked, from one end of town through the other.

That is where I grew up.

Some from the South End did succeed by going to college and living productive and success lives and some from the North End did not, but the seemingly inbred attitudes continued to exist throughout life for some. Many from both ends of town became good, hard working people who were successful in many ways. We were all people capable of giving and receiving love, capable of living life where it took us or developing paths for success and walking them. We all, or most, had a love of our hometown and worked to make it better for all. Many left town after high school and were not heard from again. The lack of good jobs and opportunity drove them away. The idea of leaving town as soon as possible was in the minds of people from both ends of town.

* * *

Sixty years ago our small town in southern Ohio was bustling with energy and every store front was busy offering anything anyone could want or need. There was every kind of business, plenty of churches of any denomination but there were more bars than churches. Sometimes, especially on the weekends, the small jail was overcrowded with those who celebrated too much Saturday evening but would be in church Sunday morning if they had slept off the effects of the alcohol they had consumed the previous evening. They knew they would be forgiven. The Scot-Irish traditions were at the core of city-wide beliefs. There were well-paying industrial jobs and plenty of jobs for those who had no specific training or for those who were just starting at the bottom of various job fields. There were wide tree-lined streets, beautiful homes with well-kept yards, and the smell of house paint was common.

On Saturday evenings every parking spot in the downtown shopping area was taken as neighbors parked and watched people come and go. Shops were open late and were busy. Small groups of residents could be seen standing in small groups simply talking and being neighborly. Youngsters who had earned a license to drive did so in large circles around the main business area as if keeping their eyes on the activities of the town or made the short drive to one of the area lakes for reasons best not talked about here.

The north and south areas of town mixed on the streets and brought about a positive sense of community and the love of it even with the difference in attitudes. Even the young people seemed to know most of those they met on the street. We were neighbors. We helped and cared for each other.

I cannot imagine a better place in which to grow to young manhood.

* * *

"I used to think I was the smartest guy in the class," Bill once wrote. He often mentioned his ability to argue an opposing idea to his college professors and was convinced he was right. I never felt that way. I knew I wasn't the smartest student in a class and never argued with my professors. I took what they said, not as gospel, but as a testimony to what they believed and let it go at that. I had my own ideas, right or wrong, and learned the difference as I grew to manhood.

Bill said he hated nature, the bugs, the creatures, the heat, the cold and that was that. While his father gave him opportunities to be in nature there was nothing there for him to enjoy. I loved nature and spent as much time in it as I could. The bugs could be bothersome but were fascinating in how they lived, reproduced, and died. I studied them as well as watching the flow of energy offered between the various plants as well as the health of the animals – the four leggeds, those with wings, and those that slithered. I especially enjoyed spiders and snakes and seemed to have a kinship with the grasses, plants of the forest, the trees and what rain patterns did to all things natural.

I grew to manhood in a loving family. I loved each member, appreciated what every relative had to teach, listened to every conversation, and learned from every mild punishment I received when I miss stepped or made a bad decision. I still remember the family gatherings held during the holidays and the warmth that was present at each. We still have some of the furniture used at those gatherings and at times I can visualize each person as they took their accustomed seats.

Bill was not so fortunate, and it seems as if he had no true love for his mother or father who he seemed to see as uneducated with little ambition. He often spoke of his siblings some who had lived successful lives and others who did not. Some had drug or alcohol problems and a sister committed suicide which became a focus of our letters during the last days of our letter writing practice. I often wondered how someone so unquestionably intelligent could not find any or little beauty within his birth family.

It was as if his head was in a box which could expand as he learned new things, but which had limits when it came to understanding things he could not grasp like consciousness or the importance of bugs or anything concerning nature or the unseen world. When it came to some things such as UFO's he would not accept their presence based on his understanding of scientific principles or the seeing of the movement of energy in trees, grasses, or other things in nature, or having contact with long dead people who brought information I felt was important to know. In effect he was looking at life through a pin hole and was not seeing its full beauty.

It was during a discussion of his sister's suicide that a conversation on that topic began. He seemed to care greatly for her as much as he cared about selected pets he once had and then lost. He said he had an interest in the subject and was inclined to act in that direction at some point.

When I returned to Ohio after several years being away, I immediately returned to college to complete an advanced degree I had left due to the availability of a job, really a dream job. As I worked on my degree I had to eat and feed my family so I took a position as an art therapist at a mental health center and as part of that I also worked at a call in crisis line program where many of the calls involved someone contemplating suicide. I offered examples of a few of those calls.

I told Bill I had always considered suicide an option and did not hold to views which came from society or the church, but also commented on the fallout that would be experienced by his spouse, his family, and others. I asked if that was the legacy he wanted.

I knew Bill lived with constant and severe pain. This I recognized as one of the reasons some people ended their own lives. Living with pain is a terrible thing that erodes life by eliminating the joy of living. With explanations of my history the tone of his letters changed which to me was a warning sign and I did my best to change his thoughts, but was that the best thing to do? I sometimes forget we all have free will and I endorse that fact of life. Maybe I over-stepped.

One of the crisis line stories I told Bill was about the young woman who called almost every night and talked with me or another worker. Her calls always were about her pending suicide by jumping out of a second story window and landing on the concrete below. After so many calls the staff had a conference and we were told to tell her to go ahead and jump out of the window. Our resident psychiatrist said, "Sometimes we have to leave our clients to God."

The rest of that story is the young woman did not commit suicide, but instead went to college, became a teacher and might have taught in the same school as Bill.

I printed an envelope, put a stamp on it, and put it in our rural mailbox and waited for a reply, but none came. Several weeks later a short note came, but its content made no sense to me. My wife read it and said Bill was saying goodbye.

I began to watch area obituaries but have not seen his name. I assume he is still alive, and I hope the pain he experienced is better and that his life is good. For a time, I missed taking time out of my self-imposed schedule to respond to his letters, but that has passed, and my life has moved on to the always changing ebbs and flows of nature.

I know Bill had the capacity to love. He loved his wife, he loved his pets, and I believe every act of love strengthens a person's connection to the unseen world. Every act of love tends to clear the fog created by the fear that has surrounded a person and many others. Every act of love brings more clarity and a keener acceptance of the ways of the universe.

Bill is a good man, but I think there must be something missing in his life. I hope he finds that missing key before his journey on this planet comes to an end.